HELL AND OHIO

HELL AND OHIO

Stories of Southern Appalachia

CHRIS HOLBROOK

▾▾▾▾▾▾▾▾▾▾▾▾▾▾▾▾

GNOMON

FIRST EDITION

Copyright © 1995 by Chris Holbrook

Library of Congress Catalogue Card Number:
95-78749

International Standard Book Number:
0-91778-60-5

The author would like to thank the following publications
where two of these stories first appeared in earlier versions:
Louisville Magazine and *Now and Then*. He would also like to
thank the Kentucky Arts Council for an Al Smith Fellowship,
which helped in the writing of this book. The characters
in these stories are fictional and any resemblance to
actual people is a coincidence.

Published by: Gnomon Press,
P. O. Box 475, Frankfort,
KY 40602-0475

CONTENTS

Hell and Ohio   1

The Lost Dog   19

Unstable Ground   35

Fire   49

First of the Month   65

Eminent Domain   79

As a Snare   95

Eulogy   115

The Idea of It   125

HELL AND OHIO

"I believe if I owned both Hell and Ohio, I'd rent out Ohio and live in Hell," Marvin says. His scissors snip around my ears. I try not to flinch when he jabs me.

Daddy brought me to Marvin for my first haircut when I was six years old. I still remember how the men waiting their turns talked and joked, how they rubbed my head after it had been burr cut and laughed, how Daddy laughed, and how it felt good when Marvin dabbed lather behind my ears like he did with the men and pretended to shave it off.

It's not changed any—the piles of hair on the floor under the chair, the shelves full of bright colored bottles, the stacks of magazines and funny books, the big round mirror behind the chair. It could be twenty years ago.

"Do you know why birds fly upside down over Ohio?" Bill Little asks.

"Tell me," I say.

"Ain't nothing worth shitting on," he says.

Everybody laughs—Bill and old Tobe Singleton and Ronnie Preston. I grin and stare at Marvin's antique haircut poster—all burrs and flattops.

Marvin wraps a hot towel around my face. I close my eyes and listen to him strop his razor.

"Any of them Buckeyes ever get smart with you?" Tobe asks.

I lift the corner of the towel. "They laugh at how I talk," I say.

"What do you do about it?" he asks.

"While they're laughing, I steal their women."

Tobe chuckles.

Marvin takes the towel. He whips lather in a mug and brushes it on my face.

Tobe starts talking basketball while Marvin shaves me. The others try to shush him, but he doesn't know any better. I just close my eyes and listen to him tell about the final game of the eighty-nine regional tournament when I scored forty points, got thirteen rebounds, and came in a hair of being recruited by the Kentucky Wildcats. This is a luxury I miss in Cincinnati. Tobe gyps me on points and rebounds, but he plays up my should-have-been Wildcat career. Someday he'll have me a jersey hanging from the Rupp Arena rafters.

I still smile when I remember the talk Daddy gave us after that game, how he praised us in one breath and cussed us out in the next. "Boys, you've played hard. Goddamn it to hell, Jimmy ain't you never heard of passing off? I'm proud of ever one of you. Todd, was your head all the way up your ass on that last play? Finest team I ever had."

I walk out of the shop smelling of after-shave and tobacco smoke. Town is filled with Saturday shoppers, and everybody I see I know. I say "hello" a dozen times before I reach my truck.

My Chevy El Camino rolled off the line the same year I was born. I call her Doris. She runs as rough as she looks, but she's a good work truck. I turn the key. The starter grinds. I hold my foot on the gas and crank her again. When she finally catches, the sound of her engine is lost in the roar of her rusted out muffler. I take a turn around the courthouse, toot my horn at a carload of schoolgirls, then head out of town in a little cloud of blue smoke.

For awhile I tool around on the back roads and listen to the radio—classic country on WKNT. I cruise slow by the mouth of Brushy Creek, then bear down through the Carbide straight stretch, pushing sixty. I slow down for the S curves at Palestine and finally pull off in the last big curve before the foot of Auglin Mountain.

I leave Doris idling by the side of the road and walk across to where the bank slopes down to the creek. The water is high and still a little muddy from the week's rain. I always expect to find bits of glass or metal, something, but I never do. The walnut tree has grown up some more, new limbs sprouting from those that were splintered and sheared off. The blackberry briars covering the bank are full of bloom.

I kneel, gather up a handful of gravel and toss them one by one into the creek. They plop into the fast moving water with hardly a splash. There's no traffic, nothing but the sound of wind in the treetops and of fast running water. It's so quiet I can barely think.

It takes me a minute to see the memorial placed at the base of the walnut tree, to recognize it for what it is—a white cross amid a bunch of artificial flowers. A purple banner with Todd's name spelled out in white is draped across it. It looks like somebody's trash washed up in a flood. The sight of it hurts me. I touch the scar above my eye.

In another minute I rise and walk back across the road. I

drive up Auglin Mountain to Highway 80, head back into town on the connector and out on Route 1. I've wound through all my old territory by the time I realize how near it is to supper, how all the relations will have rolled in for Memorial Day weekend. At Carter's Dairy Bar, I turn around and steer out toward Branham's Creek and home. I drive one-handed, as slow as the law allows.

A horseshoe thunks into the soft ground by the gate just as I'm about to step into the backyard. I hear Chuck, my brother-in-law, laughing and see my sister, Lisa, standing in her pit with the second shoe. Her two kids are playing at her feet, slapping at each other around her ankles.

Chuck yells for me to take cover, then he runs and stands before the stake Lisa is tossing at. "I'm in the clear," he yells, "throw."

Lisa's face is determined as she takes aim and lofts the next horseshoe at her husband's head. It strikes much nearer the stake, bouncing between Chuck's feet as he leaps away.

Chuck starts to look angry, but when he hears everyone else laughing, he makes a joke of it. "I guess horseshoes is a mental game," he yells.

I smell charcoal smoke and cooking meat as I cross the yard, hear the hiss of juice over hot coals. Mommy is laying hamburger patties on each of the two grills she has going. She will work until all the food has been cooked, rest while everyone else is eating, then have a hurried meal before the cleanup.

Aunt Bess intercepts me before I'm halfway across the yard. "Look who finally showed up," she says.

Mommy turns. A flicker of relief crosses her face. She smiles, but there's still a look of worry in her eyes that's not eased by the sight of her only living son safe and home in the backyard.

I hug Aunt Bess, shake Uncle Verlin's hand, and heft Lisa's little girl to my shoulder. I'm surrounded by relatives. I give Mommy a helpless look. She nods and starts toward the house with her empty platter. I take a quick look around for Daddy but don't see him anywhere. I trade smiles with Uncle Verlin.

"How you making it?" he asks.

"Doing very well," I reply.

"When you moving back?" Aunt Bess asks.

"I'm settled in for now," I say.

When I finally break away and go in the house, I find Mommy sitting by herself at the kitchen table.

"How is everything?" I ask.

"About like always," she answers. She stares at the tabletop with a sad smile. "When you coming home again?"

"Fourth of July, maybe. Labor Day for sure."

She nods, forms her mouth to say something else then doesn't. We have to work our way around the real subject.

"How's Daddy?"

She smiles faintly and motions with her head toward the living room. I hear the TV playing. "Game on?"

"There's always a game on," she says. We sit quietly for a minute, smiling and nervous. Then I say, "I guess I'd better go see him."

Daddy sits in his recliner. I'll bet it's where he sleeps most times, in front of the TV. He has a stack of sports magazines nearby and a few day's worth of newspapers. There's a plaque on the wall that shows his coaching record: 485–133. Winningest coach in the history of Caudill County High.

He mutes the TV and gets out of his chair when he sees me come in, like he didn't know I was home already. "Hey," he says. He starts to slap me on the shoulder, then he pauses and reaches for my hand, but that's not right either, so he just looks at me. "When'd you get in?" he asks.

"A while ago."

"Your Mommy never told me," he says. "She was worried, but I told her you'd be all right." He's put on weight. His face has puffed out. It's red, like he's hot, angry, and embarrassed all at once. His belly stretches his shirt front, threatening to pop buttons when he moves. He can't be healthy.

"I-75 was jammed," I say. "You'd think all of Ohio was coming home to the hills."

"About the truth," he says.

We small talk for awhile, then we both get quiet and stand facing each other. It's the same silence I had with Mommy, both of us knowing what's on each other's minds but neither being able to speak it.

I glance at the silent action on the TV screen. "Magic and Pacers?" I ask.

"Yeah," he says. He motions me to a chair, and we watch the game for half an hour without speaking. The Pacers have their defense working, and with Shaquille O'Neal in foul trouble by the end of the first quarter the momentum is theirs for this game. When Reggie Miller sinks a three pointer from near half court, Daddy slaps the arm of his chair. "Just like you used to do," he says.

"Not like that," I reply. "Not from no NBA range."

"You did," he insists, his voice rising, his face turning even redder in his excitement.

"You must be thinking of somebody else," I say. Right away I know that didn't come out the way I'd meant it.

"I guess I am," Daddy says. His face goes blank.

Our conversation dries up quick. There's not another sound until my foot slips on the floor and pops up to kick the coffee table. "Sorry," I say. Daddy just stares at the TV like there's not another person in the room.

At halftime Chuck and Lisa come in to call us for dinner. They have to coax Daddy out of his chair. "Don't be so standoffish," Chuck says. "Come out and mingle with your kinfolk."

Daddy shakes his head and sighs. "That's more of a task than you know," he says. His voice is serious.

"Daddy!" Lisa exclaims. Chuck laughs, nervously at first, then all out because he figures Daddy made a joke. I know he didn't.

We fill three picnic tables set end to end and eat like there's no tomorrow—hamburgers, hot dogs, chicken, coleslaw, potato salad, baked beans, deviled eggs, cornbread. Cousin Elgin shows up with a box full of venison steaks, and I get the first one off the grill.

"I know you don't get to eat like this very often," Aunt Bess says and spoons more coleslaw onto my plate.

"Have another hamburger," Lisa says.

"Eat some of this good cornbread," Chuck says.

"I know it's hard being so far from home," Mamaw Jesup

7

says. She reaches her hand across the table, and I reach mine to meet it. She's ninety years old, but her mind is clear, and her grip is strong on my arm.

"I'm getting by okay," I say and rub her hand to warm it.

I'm dizzy by the time I quit eating. I watch Daddy out of the corner of my eye. He sits with his head bent over a plate full of beef ribs, venison, and potato salad. He smiles when people speak to him, laughs whenever a joke is told, then gets quiet again when he's left to himself. He eats like it's a chore he has to finish.

After dinner, I sneak around the side of the house with Chuck and Uncle Verlin. We take a walk around Chuck's new/used pickup, while Chuck points out the details. "78 Explorer," he says. "302 Cleveland engine, Crager wheels, raised letter Goodyear mud-grips."

It's a good looking truck. I think about offering him an even trade on Doris, just for a joke. Chuck pulls out a pint bottle of whiskey, and the three of us settle on the tailgate of his truck to pass it around.

"Here's to family," Chuck says.

I take a quick look behind me then turn the bottle up and drink deep.

By the end of the day the visiting relatives have been shared out among various households. I lie in bed in mine and Todd's old room and listen to the house settle down for sleep. Chuck and Lisa's bedtime quarrel filters softly through the wall behind my head. Their kids yell and fight for awhile, but finally their tiredness overcomes them and they hush. Mommy rattles around in the kitchen for awhile, working herself to distraction. Daddy shuts off the TV around eleven. By midnight the house is quiet, and I'm still awake.

I reach for the lamp on the night table, snap it on, and stare for awhile at mine and Todd's trophy shelf, an army of silver and gold figures all posed in perfect layup form—one leg tucked up, one hand pushing the ball, eyes to the rim.

I was good because I out hustled everybody else, because I scrapped for every rebound or open shot, and because I was bigger and rougher than anybody else on the floor.

Todd was just good. He was as tall at sixteen as I was at eighteen, and he hadn't stopped growing. He had a smooth, graceful motion. His hands were soft on the ball, and he could shoot from anywhere on the court, open or not, standing up or falling down, with ease.

By one in the morning I give up on sleep. I get up quietly and creep down the hallway to the kitchen. I get a pop and a leftover hamburger then walk as silently as I can to the living room. The floor creaks under my feet. I pause to choose my steps, afraid of waking the whole house.

Daddy is sleeping in his recliner, so I turn on the TV with the sound off and sit on the couch to eat my snack. I watch an infommercial for some kind of hobbyhorse exercise contraption.

I think about Todd as I get sleepy. Sometimes I get him into my dreams that way. I think about him putting up jumpers from thirty feet. I see the ball turning in the air, dropping straight through the rim. I hear the whish of the net.

I must have dozed off, because the next thing I know the infommercial has turned into the morning news. I look over to see Daddy staring at me.

9

"Go inside," he says in a low voice.

I shake my head to wake up. "What?"

"Goddamn it to hell," he says. "Concentrate." And then he starts snoring again.

In the early morning, while Mommy, Lisa, and the rest of the clan go to church, Chuck, Daddy, and I go to the family cemetery to mow the grass, cut weeds, and clean up around the graves.

Daddy and I are both tired from our unsettled sleep. We ride quietly while Chuck hums along to WKNT's Sunday morning gospel show. It's turning into a humid day, and by the time we get to the cemetery and unload our lawnmower, weed eaters, rakes and hoes, we're already sweating.

Chuck heads off to the cemetery's back edge with a weed eater. Daddy begins raking up the brush, and I start on the mowing. The cemetery is on such a steep slope that I have to tie a rope to the lawnmower's handles, letting it roll downhill while it cuts, then pulling it back up with the rope. By noon we're finished with our work, and the rest of the family has arrived with the decorations.

We put new flower arrangements on half a dozen graves. The only one I dread is Todd's. It wouldn't be so bad if I was alone, but with all the rest of the family standing around, I feel like I'm being judged.

We gather at the house again for Sunday dinner before everybody takes off. I sit on the couch with Mamaw Jesup, Uncle Curtis, and Aunt Bess, quiet enough for a prayer meeting.

Mommy is in the kitchen, and Daddy is off hiding in another part of the house.

Chuck sits in Daddy's recliner and Lisa sits on the arm next to him. Their two kids wrestle across the rug. When the little boy bites the little girl on the arm, Lisa swats his head. Both children bawl. Chuck yells at them to stop crying before he gives them something to cry about.

The children don't stop. Chuck throws up his hands. He glares at Lisa. "A divorced man is a free man," he threatens and gets up to leave the room.

Lisa's face turns red. She smacks each child's hand, then walks them out to the porch, promising candy in a soothing voice.

Mamaw Jesup shakes her head. "I'd like to take over the raising of them two for about a month," she says.

"Which two you mean?" Aunt Bess asks.

After dinner the clan goes outside to rest in the shade of the big elm trees at the edge of the yard, near our old basketball court. Lisa has to drag Daddy out of the house. She leads him by one hand while her daughter, Tammy, hangs on by the other.

The evening has begun to cool off, and I'm just about to feel relaxed when Chuck comes out of the house bouncing our old basketball. "Oh no," I think. "This is just what I don't need." I try to beg off, but with the whole clan standing around what choice do I have? I look at Daddy. I can tell he wants to get away, but with Lisa and Tammy holding his hands he's as trapped as I am.

In another minute we're under the goal, choosing up. I'm on sides with Uncle Verlin and Chuck, against Daddy, Cousin Elgin, and Elgin's oldest son, Freddy. Freddy starts for Caudill County High. He's the family's newest sports hero. He shoots for possession against Chuck.

Chuck flings a hard, flat shot that caroms off the backboard, spins around the rim, and falls off. Freddy puts a high, pretty arc on his shot and drops it straight through the rim. I admire his form.

"Play to twenty-one," Chuck says.

Uncle Verlin checks the ball to Daddy. Daddy inbounds to Cousin Elgin, who puts down a fumble-handed dribble and uses his big butt to push me toward the goal. Then he pulls up, flings the ball to Freddy, and sets a pick to take Chuck out as Freddy goes around for a layup.

When they try that trick again, I make a spin move and meet Freddy under the basket. Instead of shooting he flicks it under my arm, and I look around to see Daddy backboard a shot from just under the goal.

Freddy and Daddy rack up half a dozen points before we even score. Then Elgin takes his first shot and misses. Chuck gets the rebound and throws it back out to me.

The ball is light in my hands. It's so old, worn so smooth with play, there's hardly any grain left to its skin. It's lost so much of its bounce, I can barely dribble it on the grassy court. Freddy comes out to guard me, and when I cut toward the goal, the ball takes a hop off the point of rock. It goes one way, and I go another.

They make three more goals by the time we get another possession. Elgin misses a hook, and I manage to bring down the rebound by bulling Freddy out of the way. When I take the ball outside, Freddy is in my face the whole time. His skills aren't up to mine at my best, but he's a dozen years younger than me, and I haven't played so much as a pickup game in five years.

He makes me work. The sweat begins to roll. The lungs burn a little. My head knows what to do, but from the neck down it's like I've been dipped in cement. Then, almost without realizing it, I find my groove.

I bend my knees, cock the ball just above my right eye and put up a jumper from about twenty feet. The ball falls silently through the bare rim, perfect, though I miss the satisfying snap of a net. I look at Daddy after my shot, a habit I could never break. He's smiling, just a little, and for a second I forget what's come between us.

In ten minutes the score is tied. Freddy and I trade a few points. Daddy hits a layup, and even Chuck, Uncle Verlin and Elgin manage to score. We tie up again at twenty.

Freddy guards me hard on my next possession. I manage to fake him out and am just pulling up for the game winner, an easy jumper from ten feet, when I see Daddy watching me. He's standing with his hands on his hips. He's smiling again, like I've not seen him smile in a long time. He nods his head. His mouth silently forms a single word. "Shoot."

Just that quick something goes out of whack. My hands get tight on the ball. I crouch and jump in one smooth motion, but then I hesitate and the ball sticks in my hands. I don't get it off until I'm coming down. I swear I don't mean to miss. But I do. I miss goal and all.

It takes Freddy about a second to grab up the rebound, take it out and sink a pretty little hook from about free throw distance. Then his quick jump shot wins it.

Freddy wants to play another game, but I'm done. I'm

beat. The look on Daddy's face says it all. I swear I didn't mean to miss that shot.

It's a relief when it's finally time to leave. I try not to look back as I pull out of the driveway. I know I'll see my parents on the front porch, maybe waving good-bye or maybe just watching.

Two hours into the drive I'm still thinking about Todd. There are times, when I've been away from home for awhile, that the memory will dull a little, and I'll think "This ain't so bad. I can handle this." Then I'll go home for a weekend or maybe just a day and it'll be like I'm living the whole thing over again.

I can feel the Corvette sucking down to the blacktop, gliding through the curves at Palestine without even a tire squeak. I hear myself yelling. I hear Todd's wild laughter. I taste sweet, cheap wine in my mouth.

The 'Vette was a graduation present from Daddy. It was ten years old, but even so he must have saved for a long time. I came home after that last game to find it parked in the driveway. He said he wanted to send me off to college in style.

Todd and I tore up the highways that summer. We drove all over creation—from place to place just to be on the move. We'd go to Buckhorn Lake to be seen and admired, the Prestonsburg Drive-in to drink beer and raise hell. Late at night we cruised the back roads, sipping Bourbon whiskey and screw-top wine.

I remember the quick fading of moon and stars. I remember the smell of rain, it's sudden warmth pouring down upon us through the 'Vette's open T-top roof. That's the best I've ever felt.

We'd laugh and talk, lay out futures full of parties, women—whatever we could imagine. Todd's only worry was whether he wanted to follow me to college and play with me or go to a rival school and play against me.

"It'll all be the same in the end," I told him. "All the same."

I remember Todd saying something just as we came into that last curve before Auglin Mountain. I looked at him, asked what he'd said. He was smiling, mouthing the words to some song in his head, one foot resting on the dashboard, tapping out the time, a half empty bottle of wine held between his legs. Then I saw a look of surprise flash across his face. This all happened in a heart beat.

It was some kind of animal, a deer or a big dog, standing square in the road. I braked, turned the wheel. The tires skidded on the wet road. We spun all the way around, and then we left the road. Brush and tree branches filled the headlights. We came up hard on something. The Corvette's hood shattered like an egg shell. Shards of fiberglass stung my face and hands. We rolled, once at least, but were right side up when we finally stopped.

At first I couldn't even breathe. Then when I could breathe, I looked at Todd. He was smiling, the bottle of wine still held between his legs, though it had spilled all over his shirt. "Whoooee!" I yelled and punched him in the shoulder. That's when I noticed how still he was.

I didn't make it to college that fall. After the funeral I went north and got a job working construction. I've spent the last few years framing houses, laying brick, hanging drywall. It's something else I'm good at.

It's been dark for a couple of hours by the time I reach Cincinnati. I park under a lamp post outside my building. This is not a bad street. Sometimes late at night I'll hear the drunks pouring out of the bar across the way, but it's mostly just loud talk and a little brawling. My upstairs neighbor got robbed a few weeks ago, but that's a rare occurrence. I don't worry.

My room seems even messier than I'd left it. It smells of unwashed laundry and dirty dishes. I spend a few minutes straightening up. I stuff all the laundry into a basket, stack the dishes in the sink, scare the roaches back into hiding.

It's almost an hour before I start to get nervous. I've lived in this town for five years. I've had this same room for two. Even so I can't help feeling like an inmate. I can't help needing to escape.

I go down to the sidewalk, sit on the stoop before my building and smoke a cigarette to excuse my loitering. I watch the little bar across the street, try to identify the two or three patrons huddled in the dim interior.

I wonder sometimes if I've seen Daddy or Mommy for the last time, if they'll still be living when I get home again. It's something I think about each time I make this trip.

There are times when I'm among my family or the people in the county who've known me forever, that I feel like I've lived the best part of my life already, that everything good is already behind me and there's nothing more to be had. Those times I feel like I have to get away before I smother and die. There are other times when I get so homesick I could almost cry, a time or two I have, and I know then that everything I ever cared about or ever will care about is in those hills.

My cigarette has burned down to the filter by the time I remember it. I toss the butt into the gutter and rise to walk across the street.

The barroom is dark but for the fluorescent glimmer of beer signs and the bright glare of the TV screen. I take a stool and am served a beer without having to ask. Sometimes I wonder how much of a regular I'm getting to be.

"Hey, Kentucky," somebody yells.

I look down the rail at my fellow down-and-outers, their heads bowed over glasses of beer or liquor. I see a boy I've been working with lately. I can tell by his face how lit he is.

"Hey, Ohio," I yell.

"What's a Kentucky virgin?" he asks.

"Tell me," I say.

"It's a girl who can run faster than her brother."

My fellow patrons raise their heads long enough to laugh a little. I grin and lift my glass in salute.

I stare at the TV in the corner. There's a game on of some kind. I wonder if Daddy is watching it at home. I drain my beer, signal for a refill, and try to think of a reply to Ohio's joke.

THE LOST DOG

Joe's father had put an ad in the county paper about Queenie being lost. He'd even called in to WKNT and had them announce it on the radio. He'd brought the dog home with him from some place in West Virginia as a gift to Joe, and Joe still felt like it was his fault for the dog running off and getting lost. They had about given up on finding her again when a man called from Auglin and said he'd seen the little black and tan beagle around his place.

Joe was still tying his shoes by the time his father was out the door and in the car. He had to wait on his mother to bring an extra overshirt and a heavy coat and gloves. "It's not very cold," he complained, but she looped a scarf around his neck and stretched a wool cap over his tangled hair.

Through the front window Joe could see his father sitting in the car, one arm propped on the steering wheel, the other draped across the seat back. Joe ran outside as soon as his mother let him go.

"Are you ready?" his father asked when Joe was in the car.

Joe saw the aggravation in his face. "Yeah," he said.

His father put the car in gear, and they pulled onto the road.

Joe watched the mirror on his side to see his mother go back inside. She stood for a long while in the open doorway, her arms crossed. He watched the little house, a thin trickle of coal smoke rising from the chimney, fade behind them.

"We'll stop at Clayton's," his father said when they were on the main highway. He didn't speak again until they pulled into the little grocery with its single pair of gas pumps. "Jump out and pump the gas," he said. "I'll be in the store."

Joe's breath steamed into the cold air while he filled the tank. The cold of the metal pump handle went through the cloth of his glove and chilled him even more. He was glad now of the extra clothes his mother had forced on him. After he'd pumped the gas, he watched the store for his father's return and wondered if he was supposed to go inside. He stamped his feet and clapped his hands together for a few minutes, then the cold made up his mind.

Joe's father stood before the counter, across from Mr. Clayton, tapping his finger into a large book that lay open between them. He had taken off his cap. His hair was tangled like a small boy's, and his face was red like he'd stood too long next to a heater.

At first Mr. Clayton shook his head, then he blew out his breath in a sigh, leaned over the book, and began to write. He turned the book around so Joe's father could write in it. When he was finished, Joe's father pressed his hat onto his head. "What are you waiting on?" he said as he walked past Joe. "If you're waiting on a candy bar or a pop, you might as well forget it."

Joe felt his own face redden as he followed. His father didn't speak again until they were both in the car. Then he let go with what Joe had seen in his face. Joe sat quietly while his father swore.

It had been three months since his father had quit his truck driving job and come home to stay. Joe wished now and then that he had not, that he was still coming in one weekend out of the month with jarfuls of pennies and big candy bars and toy trucks that were like the rigs he drove and cowboy hats from Texas and big shells from the ocean, but he never said anything about it.

Halfway across the county his father got over his mad spell. He started singing an old song that Joe could barely remember hearing on the radio. It was a county song about a fox, though it was not really about a fox. It was really about a boy whose girl had treated him bad and then run off, and the way she'd run off was like a fox running. Joe liked the song, and though his father singing it made him uneasy, when he stopped suddenly, like he'd just remembered Joe was in the truck, Joe wished he would start again just so there would be some noise between them.

"Maybe I shouldn't have brought you with me," his father said. "If you get sick or something happens to you, your mommy'll throw a fit."

"I'm okay," Joe replied.

At the top of Auglin Mountain they turned onto Branham's Branch for a few miles, then off onto a little nameless holler road. The houses became sparser. For long stretches there would be nothing but the bare trees and gray hillsides, then they would come upon a single house or two or three houses or trailers clumped together.

The road was deeply rutted, rising and falling with the contours of the mountain. Joe wondered how his father knew where they were going.

As if in reply, his father said, "I growed up on the other

side of that ridge." He pointed before them. "This was a main road once. I walked it many a time when I was your age, all the way into Hindman and even to Hazard."

"That must have been something," Joe said and knew at once that what he'd said had struck his father wrong.

"Don't get smart," his father said. "I'm telling you things I remember, things I'd think you'd want to know."

They turned onto an even narrower side road that was no more than a pair of tire ruts sunk so deep the car's axle could barely clear the ridge between them. The tires bounced in the uneven ruts as the car slipped and spun steadily upward for a quarter of a mile.

Joe looked off the side at the valley floor hundreds of feet below.

"Do you know right where Queenie is?" he asked.

"I know where the feller lives that called about her," his father said.

In a little while they came upon an old two-story house set just off the road on a little clearing of land. Three sides of the house were painted white. The fourth was blue. Joe wondered whether it had been planned that way or whether that had been all the paint they had had to paint it.

There was a half-acre field on one side and a barn and storage shed. Joe heard dogs barking as soon as his father stopped the car, though it took him a moment to see the kennel just within the tree line on the ridge behind the house. He smelled the hog lot as soon as he got out of the car.

A group of people stood in the field around a fire that burned beneath a big steaming kettle. Beside the kettle was a rough table made of sawhorses and heavy boards, and next to that a tripod of long, thick poles supporting a large pulley. There was an old man with a rifle and an old woman who moved around the table like she might not be old at all and two young men who stood with their hands in their pockets and a boy not much older than Joe who stood boldly in the middle of the group. A rusted out pickup truck was parked to one side.

Joe followed his father into the field.

"Howdy," the old man said as soon as they were in speaking distance.

Joe's father raised his hand and said, "We've come looking for a dog."

"A little black and tan?" the man asked.

"Was you the one who called?"

"I seen her this morning," the man said. "She's been nosing around my dogs, but she's too shy to let us catch her. Pretty little thing."

"I reckon she's still around somewheres," Joe's father said.

"She's around somewheres," the man said. He shifted the rifle from one hand to the other. They all stood quietly for a few moments and stared at each other, then Joe's father said. "You getting ready to kill a hog?"

"Getting ready to," the man said. "We're a little short of help. My oldest boy's not showed yet."

"I've not seen a hog killed in years," Joe's father said.

"You wouldn't want to help us?" the man asked. "We could spare you a few pounds of sausage if you like or souse. My wife makes the best souse you ever ate."

"I might like to help," Joe's father said. He turned his head to look at Joe. "I'm a little rusty."

"We'll get the rust off," the man said. He stepped forward

and put his hand out for Joe's father to shake. "I'm Hyram Bennet." They shook hands, and Joe's father said his name.

Joe stood quietly beside his father while the grownups talked. He was aware of the other boy staring at him, and though he glanced at the boy once or twice Joe tried not to stare back. After a while they stopped talking and walked across the field to the hog lot.

At first Joe shied away from the lot, though when the other boy jumped up on the rails, Joe stepped forward and climbed up next to him. "He's mean," the boy said loudly. He jabbed a stick at the hog then turned to look at Joe.

The hog continued to root among the litter of its pen. It had a black snout and three black hooves.

"He's mean," the boy said again and shoved his stick at the hog's eyes. It squealed loudly this time and butted its shoulder into the rails. Joe shouted and jumped back, falling to the ground. The boy and one of the young men laughed. Joe's father smiled nervously and said, "Get up from there, Joe. Be careful."

Joe got quickly to his feet, the seat of his pants smeared with mud. The other boy still hung upon the rail of the hog lot, staring over his shoulder in a way Joe thought was mean. Joe felt his face turn red and was glad of the cold air.

"He's about a five hundred pounder," said Mr. Bennet.

"I'd say," Joe's father replied.

"It's cold enough," said Mr. Bennet. "Big frost this morning."

"Oh, the weather's right," Joe's father agreed.

There was more silence as the grownups shifted their feet and looked around. The two young men lit cigarettes. The hog grunted, poking his snout through the rails. When it

24

was clear that no one could find anything more to say, Mr. Bennet stepped forward and took the boy's arm, pulling him gently from his perch on the rails. "Get off there now, Lonnie," he said. "We need to get this done."

He clicked the rifle lever and slid the barrel through the rails. Lonnie snuck back to where he could see. Joe's father, the two young men, and the woman eased a little closer, enough to watch but not distract Mr. Bennet in his task. Joe stood off to the side, unsure of what was about to happen and a little afraid.

He heard the hog grunt, and then it became quiet in an odd way. A few seconds later the rifle went off. The hog squealed wildly and battered against the rails so hard that even Lonnie backed off. Mr. Bennet said, "Damnit, I wanted to down him with that one shot."

He leaned over into the lot with the rifle as the hog thrashed and squealed and bucked drunkenly against the rails. Just when Joe was sure that the animal would break through the wooden planks, the gun shot again and the animal's commotion stopped.

One of the young men backed the rusted out pickup to the pen. The other opened the gate. They made a ramp from the truck bed to the floor of the hog lot with a pair of two-by-fours and tied ropes around the hog's body, then all of the men, Joe's father included, manhandled the dead hog into the bed of the truck.

They backed the truck to the table beside the big boiling pot and rolled the hog out onto the sawhorse table. The old woman dipped boiling water from the pot and poured it over the hog's body, then she and the two young men went to work with long knives, scraping away the rough hair.

Joe watched for a while, then his father came to him and said, "Joe, I'm going to go have a look around for Queenie with Mr. Bennet. You'll be okay till I get back?"

It was more an order than a question, so Joe nodded his head that he'd be fine. He watched uneasily as his father and Mr. Bennet walked away. When they were gone, Lonnie nudged Joe with his elbow and asked whether he'd ever seen a hog killed before.

Joe said he hadn't, and Lonnie looked at him in wonderment. "Why not?" he asked.

"I don't know," Joe said. "I've just not."

"Don't you raise hogs?" Lonnie asked.

"We never have," Joe said.

They fell silent as they watched the work. The two young men worked slowly and were sloppy. They took breaks to talk or smoke their cigarettes and left patches of bristle on the pale flesh of the carcass. But the old woman was an expert. The hog's coarse hair fell in clumps from her knife blade to the ground, and only clean skin was left behind.

After a few minutes Lonnie nudged Joe again. "What's your daddy do?" he asked.

Joe could hear his father's voice calling out the name of their dog. "He's a truck driver," Joe said, "but he quit."

"Quit? What'd he quit for? That sounds like a good job. I'd like to be a truck driver."

Joe shrugged his shoulders.

"I'll bet he got fired," Lonnie said.

"No, he just quit."

"What's he do now?"

Again, Joe shrugged his shoulders. His father's voice became more distant.

"I'll bet he got fired," Lonnie said. "I'll bet he got fired and then they blacklisted him and now he can't find no job nowhere. I'll bet that's what it is."

"That's not it," Joe replied. He paused and thought about what had been said between his mother and father. His father had been promised a job in the mines at Yellow Creek because he was friends with the foreman there, but something had happened at the mine, a layoff, before he could start work, and now he just had to wait and see because he'd already quit his job driving trucks.

"I'll bet he didn't quit," Lonnie insisted. "I'll bet he was fired."

Joe remembered what his mother had said about his father coming home to stay, about how they were going to get by until he got another job, and about how they had to get used to living with one another again. He wanted to be able to explain it.

"Hey," Lonnie shouted. "What's that?"

Joe looked to the hillside where Lonnie pointed, and as soon as he did felt Lonnie's hands on his coat collar and something wet and rough on the back of his neck. Joe tried to fight free, but Lonnie was stronger and held on until he'd shoved whatever it was down Joe's back. Joe felt prickles like tiny needles against his skin. He danced around to shake them loose, but the more he moved, the more they spread and itched. Lonnie laughed out loud, and even the two young men and the old woman grinned a little. Joe felt tears rising to his eyes. When he saw his father hurrying across the field, he stopped dancing and shouted in a choking voice. "He put something down my neck."

"Just hog bristles," Lonnie said, smiling slyly.

"It's just a joke," Joe's father told him, and he pulled up the back of Joe's coat and shirt to dust the coarse hairs from his back. "It's just a joke somebody always pulls. You're too big to cry over a joke."

Joe wiped his face on his coat sleeve and took deep breaths to slow his crying, and in a little while he was better.

"It's time to haul him up," Mr. Bennet said.

They threaded a cable through the pulley on the tripod, hooking one end to the truck's back bumper and the other to the hog's back legs. Then one of the young men drove the pickup slowly forward and hoisted the hog from the table. When the hog was in position, the old woman set a large tub beneath its head.

"Who wants to let the blood?" Hyram asked.

"I will," Joe's father said, "if I remember how."

He took one of the knives and knelt by the hog's head. He seemed to study for a minute, then he made a cut on the hog's throat, and blood began to pour into the tub.

"Do better than that," Mr. Bennet said, "cut its head off."

"I'm going to sit in the car," Joe said, though no one paid him any attention. He felt his stomach surge into his throat with each slash of the knife against the hog's flesh. He tried to look away, but he could still hear the sound of the cutting. He covered his mouth with his hand and said louder, "I'm going to sit in the car."

"Go on," his father said, "if you have to."

Joe ran across the field toward the car, taking big gulps of air through his mouth to ease the rising sickness. He felt better once in the car, though he could still smell the hog. Its scent rose from his clothes and burned in his nostrils. For a little while he kept an eye on the activity, though when

Mr. Bennet opened a cut down the hog's center, spilling out its tub full of guts, he had to fight again to keep from gagging.

It was when he looked away that he saw the small black and tan beagle on the hillside across the road. Ragged and starved looking, she stood motionless, attentive to the hog slaughter, her nose raised to sniff the air.

Joe thought to go for his father, though when he looked, he saw his father and Mr. Bennet on either end of a crosscut saw, halving the hog's body down its spine. Instead, he eased the car's door open and took a step toward the frightened dog.

At first she stood still while Joe approached, but when he was within a few yards she whined and took a step away. Joe had come close enough to see her matted fur and the cuts that covered her body. She had fought something or been tangled up in something sharp. "She's hurt," Joe thought. "That's why she's shy."

Joe hunkered down a little and held out his hand. He clicked his tongue and called out the dog's name. "Here, Queenie. Come on girl. Come on."

Queenie cowered onto her haunches. She growled a little and backed off a little more. Joe continued to move forward, on his knees now, through the brown winter grass and weeds. He kept one hand before him and called softly, "Queenie. Queenie."

Queenie whimpered and rose to her feet, but neither ran away nor came to Joe's call. When he was in reaching distance, Joe stopped and remained very still. He spoke to her for a long while so that she might recall his voice or his scent, though that would now be covered by hog scent.

29

When a sudden noise startled her, Joe knew she had turned more afraid now than trusting. Before she could run, he made a lunge and caught her.

Joe knew the rough handling hurt the already injured dog, but he also knew that if he let go she would run off and then might die. He held on tightly and spoke softly. "I'm sorry," he said.

Queenie howled and struggled to free herself. Joe could feel her heart beating in fright, her body trembling. He held his hand before her snout. After she had sniffed it for a moment and recognized his scent beneath the strong smell of hog, she began to calm, though she still whimpered as Joe half carried and half dragged her back to the car. He called to his father who jogged quickly across the field.

"I caught her," Joe said.

His father lifted Queenie and laid her gently in the car's back seat. He petted her head and spoke to calm her down. Queenie whimpered just a bit more, then she meekly wagged her tail and curled up to lick the wounds that covered her flank.

"I wonder what she got into," Joe's father said.

Before they left, Mr. Bennet thanked Joe's father for his help and told him to come back in a few days after the hog had been butchered and his wife had made the souse. Joe's father said he would, then he and Joe got in the car and started off.

They rode quietly for a while. Joe waited for his father to say something about him catching Queenie. What he finally said was, "It's not your fault you can't do much, Joe. You've not been taught."

Joe didn't speak.

"I've not been around much," his father said.

Joe wanted to tell how he'd caught Queenie and to ask if his father thought Queenie would be all right and what they ought to do to fix her up. "That's okay," he said, but his father seemed not to hear him.

"Things are up in the air right now," he said. "I don't know what's going to happen. I might have to go back to long hauling."

Joe watched the wintry sky, the bare trees, and gray hillsides. He thought about the jarfuls of pennies his father used to bring in from his trips.

His father let go of the car's steering wheel and motioned with his hands. "If I could stay close to home and be with you and your Mommy ever minute, I would," he said. "If it's up to me, I will."

His father stopped the car at the top of the steep hill they had crossed earlier. He sat for a long time, staring straight ahead. "There's things you need to learn," he said. "Things I need to teach you." He put the gear shift into park and set the brake, then he got out and walked around to Joe's side of the car and opened the door.

"Slide over," he said.

"What?" Joe asked.

"Drive this thing," his father said. He got in and nudged Joe across the seat until he was behind the wheel.

"The first thing you do," his father said, "is put your foot on the brake, then you let off the emergency and put it in gear."

Joe looked down the hill before them. It seemed narrower and steeper than when they had come up it. He looked over the side into the valley. He looked at his father.

31

"Drive," his father said.

Joe had to slide down in the seat for his feet to reach the pedals. He pressed both feet onto the brake, let off the emergency, and pulled the gear shift into drive.

"Go on," his father said when the car didn't move. "Drive."

Joe eased his feet off the brake, and the car started down the hill. He could feel the road fighting his hands on the wheel as the car gathered speed. When he touched the brake pedal again, the car slid on the loose dirt and rocks. It swayed from side to side, the underside scraping bare stone and earth, then it bounced high and headed toward the edge of the road. Before Joe could react, his father's hand was on the wheel, steering the car back into the center.

"Just point it straight," his father said.

Joe held tight, his teeth jarring, his heart pounding, his breath coming short. A frightened whine came from the back seat, and Joe glanced in his mirror to see Queenie curled into a ball, her eyes restless and bright. The car bounced once more on a large rock. There was a sound of metal scraping stone, then a loud, steady roar from the undercarriage.

At the bottom of the hill, Joe stopped the car. He put the shift into park, set the brake, and let the engine idle. His father sat with his arms crossed, staring straight ahead. Joe couldn't tell from his face if he was angry, though he knew he must be because of how the car sounded now. He waited for his father to tell him what he'd done wrong.

After a little while Joe's father turned to him. When he spoke his voice was the mildest it had been all day. "That's good for a start," he said. "Keep going."

Joe put the car in gear and drove slowly down the holler road. He kept to the center, and after a while learned to steer without swaying. Before long he learned not to mind the feel of his muddy clothes or the smell of the hog that lingered in his nostrils or the itch of its bristles on his neck.

UNSTABLE GROUND

Estill Kidd sat in his porch swing and studied the mudslide that had carried a small pine into Kermit Strong's backyard. He'd seen the makings of the slide over a year ago, when Kermit had first bought the land from Leon Thacker and begun his strip job at the head of the holler. He could have said something then, but it wasn't for him to tell another man his business.

As it was, Estill had barely spoken to Kermit in a year. They had last talked when one of Kermit's bulldozers had run a few feet across Estill's property line. No real harm had been done, and Estill had gone to see Kermit only as a matter of principle.

Kermit had heard him out without speaking, then told Estill that he was sorry and for him to submit an estimate for damages. Estill had said to hell with it and tried to ask how the work was coming. Kermit had walked away while Estill was still talking.

A week later Estill had received a check in the mail for a hundred dollars. When he'd tried to take it back, Kermit had refused, and Estill had come away feeling like he'd been caught in some thievery.

Estill had known Kermit's father nearly forty years, longer than Kermit had been in the world. They had dug in the

35

same mines, raised their families and built up their homes in the same community. Estill could still recall the brand of cigar he and Vernon had smoked at Kermit's birth. He could name no fault in the man, and he could not account for the difference between father and son.

Over the next few months he'd sat back and watched the commotion. First, Kermit had run his access road through the middle of the old Thacker homeplace, taking out the barn and house and ruining the pasture.

Then, when the coal started rolling out of the holler at forty dollars a ton, he'd had the slope below the access road leveled for a house seat and moved in a doublewide trailer.

Estill marveled at the foolishness of living on unstable ground. His own house was built of hand-hewn logs and rough lumber. Moss grew on the logs and on the battered split-shingle roof. It was plain, but it sat on a solid bench of earth and rock a good fifty yards higher on the mountain than the big foreign looking doublewide, which Estill saw sliding into the creek after a year or two more of hard weather.

"I don't know," Estill would say to the boys down at Buddy Collins' store. He'd shake his head and laugh a little. "It's none of my business, I guess." But the constant blasting that sent trembles through his house from foundation to eaves, rattling his cupboards and jarring his windowpanes, kept him more on edge than he would say.

Kermit had moved in just a few weeks earlier with his wife, Ida, and their little daughter, Rebecca. Ida's parents were members of Estill's church. She had grown up on Right Fork, and Estill had known her since she was a child. He could see her image in the plump, pretty little girl.

It was Ida who came out of the doublewide just as Estill was about to be driven indoors by the morning damp. She trod across the soggy yard in house slippers and a knee-length leather coat with fringes on the sleeves and metal studs that gleamed even in the gray light of the rainy morning. She lit a cigarette as soon as she was outdoors. Kermit came out as she stood looking at the uprooted pine.

Estill couldn't hear what they said, but from the way Kermit stood—staring up at the slipped hillside, his hands in his pockets—Estill could tell Ida was laying down the law about something. Her hands chopped the air, and once, when her voice rose loud enough, Estill thought he heard a swear word. He wondered at the harshness of Ida's disposition. He had known her to be such a sweet little girl.

After a while she flung her cigarette at the freshly seeded lawn and stalked back into the trailer, leaving Kermit to stare at the mess of brush and mud and upturned rock that had spilled into his newly leveled yard.

Estill sat in his porch swing, watching the rain drip from the roof edge and trying to recall the children he had known these people to be.

When the sun broke later that morning and Estill's knees began to warm, he took up his cane to walk the mile and a half to Buddy Collins' store.

Another slide had blocked two lanes of Highway 80 at the base of Sassafras Mountain. A few square-shaped boulders had tumbled from the cliff-face left by the road cut, and gravel-sized stone and muddy water still sluiced down the cliff-face and across the road.

As Estill crossed to the other side, a pair of coal trucks and a flatbed hauling a dozer came over the rise. He walked along the median while they sped down the steep grade, building momentum for the next incline.

The coal trucks rode side by side, almost seeming to race, the flatbed running full out on their bumpers. One of the coal trucks blared its horn as it rumbled past, and Estill stepped back from the black water that sprayed from its huge wheels. By the time they topped the next hill, they were rolling almost as slow as Estill was walking.

Buddy Collins' bare little store sat just below the crest of Sassafras Mountain, a hundred yards off Highway 80 on a little two lane strip of potholed blacktop that had once been the main road. It was empty except for Buddy, who sat behind his counter reading a newspaper. Estill claimed the high backed rocker that sat facing the door and stretched his legs before Buddy's kerosene heater. When he was settled in, he said, "What's new up your way?"

"Not a thing," Buddy replied.

Estill sat quietly for awhile, watching the shimmer of warm air above the heater. When his foot slipped on the worn wooden floor and lightly jarred the heater's metal housing, he imagined Buddy scowling at him from over his newspaper. He didn't speak again until he heard the sound of a page being turned. "That Kermit had a fine mess this morning," he said.

"What's that?" Buddy asked.

"That Kermit," Estill said. "Half the hill slid off on him."

"You don't say," Buddy replied, and Estill could hear the crumple of the newspaper being folded.

"I seen it coming," Estill said. "You'd think a grown man would have better sense than to live in such a place."

"Now, he's got a fine trailer," Buddy said.

"I don't mean to run nobody down," Estill said. "Everybody's got their own ways, but that Kermit and Ida. You never heard such a commotion as them people make, cussing and fighting. Why that Ida cussed Kermit a blue streak this morning." He hushed as the front door screeched open, and Kermit Strong walked in, Rebecca cradled on his hip.

The little girl had her mother's curly yellow hair, fair skin, and blue eyes. Not a single feature, even to her smiles and frowns, tied her to Kermit with his sharp face, straight brown hair and black eyes. It made Estill wonder.

"Gentlemen," Kermit said in a sort of raised whisper, the floor barely squeaking as he crept across it. Rebecca's head was drooped on his shoulder, her eyes half closed.

"Hello, Kermit," Buddy said, his own voice hushed so as not to rouse the sleepy child.

Estill simply nodded.

"How's you and yours?" Buddy asked.

"Scraping by," Kermit said. "About as good as can be expected." He settled Rebecca onto the counter. "This one's a little cranky this morning."

"Why she's her mother made over," Estill said, his voice louder than he'd meant it to be. Rebecca whimpered a little, grinding the heels of her hands into her eyes.

Kermit patted her back, and she drooped her head against his shoulder again. "I hope not," he replied.

"Well she is," Estill said. When Kermit didn't speak, he said, "I see where you had a little slip, this morning."

39

"I've had some slippage," Kermit said.

"You might do well to go up the mountain a ways and doze off some of that overburden," Estill said.

Kermit rolled his eyes at Buddy, then he turned a tight-lipped smile to Estill.

Estill paused for a moment, unsure what to make of Kermit's expression. "It's only going to get worse on you," he continued.

Estill couldn't hear what Kermit said under his voice. But when Buddy laughed a little, Estill knew he was being made light of. "You picked a poor house seat," he snapped as he rose from his chair. He heard Kermit's barely muffled laughter as he walked out the door. "Snicker and grin," he mumbled to himself.

Estill walked halfway home, his cane held club-like in his fist, before the ache of his knee joints overcame his anger. "If I had my way," he said aloud, easing onto a guardrail to rest, "I'd run such like out of the country."

He didn't begrudge a man showing ambition. He'd turned a few dollars on coal and timber, and he'd worked in the mines, underground and on the surface, but there was a difference. Every tree he'd cut, he'd grieved over. Every ton of coal he'd mined he'd known the trade-off for. There was a difference in this latest generation.

He thought of his own son, how he'd made his life in another place, married a woman whose family Estill had never met, and returned home less and less. He'd seen him hardly at all since his mother's funeral. They were near strangers then. Estill wondered if they would even know each other now.

"This latest generation," he muttered, then his attention was caught by a pile of beer cans littering the ditch line.

He unbuttoned his coat, unfolded a plastic grocery bag from the bib of his overalls, and stepped carefully into the muddy ditch. He worked slowly, first emptying the cans of ditch water, then setting them on the edge of the pavement to crush beneath his foot. He had cleared the roadway of nearly a dozen cans when he heard the roar of a car and looked up to see a can flying toward him. It landed at his feet, splattering its contents on his pants leg. He watched the car fishtail down the highway, the blare of its horn mixed with youngish laughter as the rogues made their getaway.

"...has forgot where it's come from," he yelled in completion of his thought. He walked the rest of the way home, smelling of beer.

A few days later Estill heard the close-by rumble of heavy machinery and walked onto his porch to see Kermit maneuvering a bulldozer around the crumbling hillside. He watched as if he had made the work happen.

"I told him what he needed to do," he thought, but Kermit stopped the bulldozer later that evening after little more than removing the recent slippage and extending his yard ten feet to a sheer cut-bank.

Kermit was just climbing off the dozer when Estill walked into the yard. He shook his head when he saw Estill approach.

41

"You ain't through, are you?" Estill asked.

"What do you mean?" Kermit replied.

"Go on up the hill," Estill said, pointing at the hillside above the cut-bank.

"I've done all I intend," Kermit said.

"They's more going to slip," Estill said.

"I'm aware of that," Kermit replied.

"Well then."

"Estill," he said, suddenly, "let's get down to it. I'll give you fifteen thousand, mineral rights and surface."

At first Estill made no reply, unsure of Kermit's meaning.

"Fifteen thousand," Kermit said, "now that's for the top and what's under it."

Estill felt a tightening in his chest when he finally understood what Kermit was about. "I'm not selling," he said, surprised at the desperate sound of his own voice.

"You could go live with that boy of yours," Kermit said.

"I'll not," Estill said. He left quickly, afraid of further talk.

On Saturday, Estill made his usual trip to the Right Fork graveyard. It had been the main graveyard for the Right Fork community until the new highway had come through and scattered the people. There had not been a burial there since his wife passed on, and he was the only regular visitor anymore, though there were some Joneses who came over from West Virginia on Decoration Day and a few Thornsberrys and Fairchilds up from Tennessee.

The graveyard was in walking distance of Estill's house, on a hillside one ridge over from Kermit's strip site. Estill was not worried for its sake. He didn't think even Kermit's ambition would go so far as to turn the dead from their graves.

Estill cleared his wife's grave of its litter of fallen leaves, then he straightened the wreath of artificial flowers he'd placed there in May. He dragged a fallen tree branch from Rebecca Fairchild's grave. He made an effort to right the stone of Alonzo Kidd. It had sunk into the ground in such a way that it seemed ready to tip over, though when he heaved against it the cold stone was as solid in the moist earth as if set in cement.

The farther he hiked up the hill, the older the gravestones became. The very oldest were simple chunks of rock, their roughly chiseled inscriptions too weathered to read. For a long while he puzzled over a small, sunken plot of ground at the graveyard's edge, running names and faces through his head.

At the sound of thunder, he looked up. A few storm clouds lingered from the past week, but the sky was mostly clear. When the thunder sounded again, louder, and the ground trembled very slightly beneath his feet, Estill knew he'd been fooled by the blasting from Kermit's strip site.

He thought to hike on up the ridge and view the site, but the cold of the day and the dull ache of his knees urged him toward home. Before he left, he paused once more by his wife's grave to see that all was as it should be.

That night he called his son.

"I cleaned off your mother's grave today," he told him. He told him of Kermit Strong's strip mining and described the new trailer, told him what all had changed in the landscape.

From his son he learned that work was good, the wife was

fine, and they might visit in the summer if they got the chance.

For two solid months, six days a week, coal trucks rolled out of the holler. The blast of dynamite and the roar of heavy machinery became constant, daylight to dark. Then from dark to daylight, it seemed, Kermit and Ida kept up a riot of squabbling. Ida would often leave for days at a time, deserting both husband and child. Estill had heard the rumors at Buddy Collins' store that Ida was running with other men.

Throughout the spring Kermit busied himself with add-ons to the trailer. He paved the driveway in front and built a deck in back. He put up a swing set for Rebecca. She would sit in a swing or on the top of the slide and watch Kermit mow the lawn or cut weeds on the hillside.

Sometimes in the afternoons when she and Kermit weren't fighting, Ida would come onto the deck in her bathing suit. She would lie in a lounge chair, smoke cigarettes, and bake in the hot sun. Estill stayed indoors on those days.

Estill's house bore the end of winter poorly. His tap water began to smell of gas; he was certain that Kermit's mining had fouled his well. His windows and doors seemed not to fit their frames and would barely open or close. One morning in early May, he heard a loud pop and found a crack running the width of his kitchen ceiling.

"I ought to law you," he said to Kermit when he saw him in Buddy Collins' store.

Kermit was sitting in Estill's usual chair. Rebecca balanced on his knee while she ate a stick of peppermint candy and studied the pages of a story book. "Law me?" Kermit scoffed.

"How old is that house? Seventy-five or a hundred? Don't blame me." As Estill turned to leave, Kermit yelled. "Think about my offer. We could both make out."

That evening Estill called his son and told him how Kermit was trying to force him from his land.

"How do you mean?" his son asked.

Estill told how his water had gone bad, about the cracks in his ceiling and the misfit of doors and windows, as if the house itself had gone off kilter.

"It's an old house," his son said.

"It always was solid before this year," Estill snapped.

"I wish I could help," his son said.

Estill let him off the phone after a long pause in which neither could find anything more to say.

On his next visit to the graveyard, Estill left his cane resting upon his wife's headstone, found a branch to use as a staff, and hiked to the ridge top to view Kermit's strip site.

Less than a hundred yards past the graveyard's edge he came upon a small trench of sunken earth. He might have missed it had he not been looking for such signs. A little further on he came upon a small maple that had uprooted.

There was more erosion near the top of the hill. Several trees had fallen. Others had lost enough soil from about their roots to begin tilting downhill. Estill soon saw what he had suspected.

One ridge had been taken off and a few acres of hillside laid bare. Kermit had stayed within his boundaries, but his activity had changed the natural slope of the hill. It had begun to slip on Estill's side.

He took a long while coming down, careful of falling on the steep slope. The graveyard seemed undisturbed as yet, though it was overgrown with weeds. Estill resolved to mow it before Decoration Day. He spent almost an hour by his wife's grave. She had been gone nearly ten years, and he could not clearly think how he had lived in that time.

He got home just before dark. Now that he had seen the slide at the ridge top, he was certain his house looked off balance. The chimney seemed to dip. The porch no longer seemed level.

By the middle of summer the strip site began to slow its activity. The more time Kermit spent at home, the more he and Ida argued. On a bright Monday morning in July, after a weekend of uproar, Ida marched out of the trailer in a fit of cigarette smoke and cursing. She threw two suitcases in the trunk of the red car Kermit had bought her, strapped Rebecca in the front seat, and drove away.

Kermit came home from his half day's work to find the open trailer door swinging in the summer breeze. That same night he drove off in his pickup. Two weeks later he returned and emptied a pistol into the doublewide. Afterwards, whenever Estill saw him in the daytime, he looked like a man on the verge of some violence.

Estill told his son of the situation.

"If I sell, I'll have money," he said. "I won't be a burden. I just need a place to go to."

His son paused a long while before answering. "Okay," he said at last. Estill heard in the tone of his voice no note of welcome.

The next day Estill found Kermit sitting on his deck, his feet propped on a cooler, his cap pulled over his eyes. His pistol and a box of shells lay within reach of his chair. "Have one," Kermit said. He held out a can of beer as Estill walked up.

Estill waved his hand. "I'm here to talk business," he said.

Kermit smiled and opened the beer for himself.

"I'll sell," Estill said.

Kermit shifted in his chair. "The fact of the matter is," he said. "I've filed chapter seven."

"I don't know what that means," Estill said.

Kermit shrugged. "I've gone under," he said. "I'm bankrupt." He lifted his cap and replaced it at a different angle then picked up his pistol and fired twice at the hillside above them.

Estill stood silently, leaning upon his cane. He stared at the swing set, the bolts already streaking rust down the white poles, the seats of the swings brushing the grass that had grown tall after weeks of neglect. "That's it then," he said. He walked home to the sound of Kermit's pistol shots.

Within a month the doublewide had been repossessed. It was rumored that Kermit had moved to Indiana in search of factory work. Ida was said to have run off to Florida with an insurance salesman, dragging Rebecca with her.

By day Estill stalked his property, searching for new signs of slippage. He found a split in one of the logs just above the foundation. He saw that the roof had begun to sag. More cracks appeared in the ceiling and walls.

He carried water from a pure tasting spring he'd found on

47

a far hillside to avoid the gassy smelling liquid that spurted from his kitchen tap. At night he stirred nervously if the floorboards popped or the wind cracked a branch against the roof. He lay awake and waited for his house to tumble from its foundations.

FIRE

Lee watched the glow of fire on the dark hillside, the flaming red and yellow ring eating downward from the ridge top. He smelled the smoke, heard the distant voices of the men.

At the slap of the kitchen screen door, he turned, saw his mother standing in the yard, hands on hips. For a moment, she and Lee locked eyes, then they both turned their gaze to the burning hills.

The fire ring broke apart a little at a time. They could almost see the shadows of the men shoveling on dirt, flailing charred feed sacks, beating the flames to death with hoes and rakes and the heels of their boots.

When the fire glow died down and all that remained in the night air was the heat and smell of smoke, the men began to come home, their tools clinking tiredly against the ground as they emerged from the ghostly, smoky tree line.

"Run bring a jug of water," Lee's mother commanded, and Lee hurried past her into the kitchen, pulling two quart jars of half frozen water from the freezer, the jars chilling his hands and his chest where he held them to him.

A half dozen people had gathered in the yard. Amos Jr. and Doc, Lee's brothers, knelt and stared tiredly at the ground. Lester Patrick and Jake Ritchie stood with hands on hips, looking back into the hills. Lee's father, Amos Sr., his mother, Clara, and his Uncle Curtis stood to one side, heads bent, talking among themselves.

"Is the fire all out?" Lee asked, handing a jug of water to his father. His father passed the jug to his brother. "Lee," he said, "take a jug to Les and Jake." His father's hands and arms were black with soot. His face was smudged, the smell of smoke all about him.

Lee moved away to offer water to Lester Patrick and Jake Ritchie.

"If people would wait past six o'clock, till the wind dies down," Lester Patrick was saying.

"It ain't just brush fires getting loose," Jake Ritchie replied.

Lee handed the water jar to Jake who smiled and laid his hand on Lee's shoulder and squeezed. "That's a good man," he said, sipping deeply from the jar then passing it to Lester.

"Is the fire all out?" Lee asked, but the men were too absorbed in their talk and water to answer. Lee wandered across the yard to where his brothers, Doc and Junior, and his cousin Donnie sat. Junior had stretched out on the dry grass. Doc was placing a lump of snuff behind his lip. "I'd like to know who's setting these fires," Donnie was saying.

"Is the fire all out?" Lee asked.

"If it ain't, I say let it burn," Doc replied.

"That's what I say," Junior added. His voice was hoarse, and he was rubbing the backs of his hands into his eyes. A smudge of soot had given him half a mustache. "Didn't bring us no water?" he asked.

"Forgets us all the time," Doc said.

Junior rolled onto his side. He coughed for nearly a

minute, his face turning red with the effort. "Dadburn," he said when he had control of himself. "Dadburnit, Lee...."

But Lee was already headed for another water jar. He paused just at the kitchen door, looking back at his family and neighbors gathered in the yard, silent now, all gazing up at the hills. He turned his face to the slight wind that still stirred, even so late in the evening, and took a deep breath of the warm, smoky air.

The tractor moved slowly across the bottom, pulling the baler over the rows of cut hay, the baler scooping the hay up at one end, dropping it out in neatly tied bundles at the other. Lee stood on the hitch, holding to the back of the tractor seat and to his father's shirt which was damp with sweat. Curtis drove behind in his pickup, pulling the hay wagon. Doc and Junior walked alongside, tossing the bales up to Donnie who hurriedly stacked them on the wagon.

From time to time, Lee's father would turn to see that Lee was still on board. He would nod, and Lee would nod and hold back the smile he felt for the ride.

At the end of the bottom, when the tractor bounced on a hump in turning, Lee slipped a little from his perch. Lee's father saw. He stopped the tractor, took Lee's arm, and set him on the ground.

Lee glanced around, then he bent over and peered underneath the tractor, as if checking for damage, but then his father motioned him away. The tractor lurched forward, and Lee was left to follow uselessly beside the baler. He touched the fresh bales with his foot, turned them over, inspecting the ropes, then he picked one up, the coarse ropes digging

51

into his hands as he half carried half dragged it to the wagon. He got it halfway on, then it fell, and he had to pick it up again and wrestle it back up. He would've lost it once more if Doc hadn't grabbed one end and flipped it on. "Watch out now, Lee," he said.

"I got a good job for you, Lee," Donnie shouted.

"Lee's got a good job," Doc said. "Who you think's the foreman of this crew?"

"I've got a job that only he can do," Donnie replied. He leaned down from the wagon, reaching his hand to Lee. "Climb up on top and weigh these bales down."

Donnie pulled Lee up into the wagon and helped him to the top of the hay stack. Lee sat, much higher than he had been on the tractor, and rode with the jostling sway of the wagon and hay load. His brothers grinned up at him as they tossed bales to Donnie, and Lee grinned back, balancing himself on the swaying, jostling hay.

They went through nearly an entire row like that. Lee laughing sometimes, and Doc and Amos Jr. and Donnie laughing when he did. Donnie stacked the bales as quickly as Doc and Junior threw them to him, packing them tightly, exactly, so that they fit on the wagon as snug as puzzle pieces. They stacked higher and higher, and soon Donnie was standing on the wagon's end, near to being crowded off altogether. Lee crawled across the stacks, trying to spread himself over the load. Donnie smiled up at him, his face red and sweating.

Just before the end of the row, the wagon bounced in a rut. The load shifted, and Lee slid off the side, grasping wildly at the hay bales, bringing the highest layer off with him. He hit the stubbled ground flat on his back, all the wind rushing from his body. He lay unmoving, trying to scream or cry, but he could neither breathe nor make a sound. Then Donnie was leaning over him, his face rigid, his hands passing over Lee's arms and legs, pressing against his chest, shaking him. Lee caught his breath with a hoarse, choking cry and began to gulp air wildly. He kept crying, even when he saw the men standing around him.

He kept crying when his father picked him up and set him on his feet. He kept crying until his father said, "hush." "Hush, Lee," his father repeated. "Hush, you're all right." When he stopped crying, he was more ashamed than afraid. His father dusted him off and wiped his face with the bandanna he had around his neck, and Lee tasted his own tears mixed with his father's sweat.

Curtis muttered a curse at Donnie. "You ought to know better than to let him up on the wagon," he said. "What's wrong with you?" Donnie stood with his hands clenched at his sides, staring at the ground, then he raised his eyes and glared hard at Lee. "I can't do nothing with no little kids around," he said.

"Junior, take Lee on home," Lee's father said, and Junior took Lee's hand and led him back toward home. When Lee looked back, he saw Curtis pulling Donnie by the arm toward the spilled hay bales.

Lee rose to the sound of his parents' voices. "Another weekend gone," his father said. Then he heard his mother shush him and his father laugh loudly and brightly.

Lee smelled sausage frying and coffee and slowly baking biscuits. He crawled quietly from the bed he shared with

53

Junior, stepped around the roll-away that Doc had to himself and left the bedroom, disturbing neither brother.

He heard his parents talking more quietly now, the hush of their voices causing him to move more cautiously through the house.

The floor creaked beneath Lee's feet just as he reached the kitchen door, and his parent's voices stopped abruptly. Lee paused, then entered the kitchen. His father sat at his place at the table, slumped carelessly in his chair, a half empty coffee cup on the table before him. His mother stood at the sink, tightening the lid on a thermos, then packing it into a lunch box.

"Well look who's up," Lee's father said.

His mother glanced at him, closing the latches on the lunch box and setting it on the table within her husband's reach. She went to the stove, opened the oven door and peeked inside.

Lee took a cup from the dish rack on the sink and poured it half full of coffee, filling it the rest of the way with tap water. He climbed into a chair opposite his father and sat blowing into the cup. His mother stood over the stove, forking sausage patties onto a plate from a still sizzling cast iron skillet, then mixing flour and cream into the leftover grease for gravy.

They were all silent for a long time, then Lee's father leaned forward and dropped a ring of keys on the table. "Lee, you feel like warming up my truck?"

Lee grinned and snatched up the keys. He took his cup of coffee, cooled and thinned with tap water, and hurried outside to climb into the cab of his father's pickup. Setting the coffee cup on the dash, he slid off the seat far enough to press in the clutch. He checked the parking brake, pulled the gear shift into neutral, then fit the key in the ignition and started the engine.

He switched on the radio and listened to the early morning farm reports from Lexington, talk about tobacco mold and prices from men who sounded like they had just met for morning coffee. No one in the mountains grew tobacco. Lee had never seen a single field, but the talk was familiar. The sound of the men's voices mixed with the thrum of the truck engine and the warm coffee and the early morning air made Lee so comfortable that by the time his father came from the house, lunch box swinging in his hand, mining cap perched on his head, he had almost gone back to sleep.

Doc and Junior came out of the house too, their clothes half buttoned, their hair still tousled, yawning while their father gave them instructions. Lee slid from the truck and hurried to join them. His father dropped a hand onto his head while he talked. "Curtis is going to need help clearing his garden this evening. Be careful the wind's died down if you burn it off."

Then he was gone in the truck that Lee had started for him, and Lee was following his sleepy brothers into the house to the smell of coffee and sausage, hot biscuits and gravy.

Curtis showed up in the late afternoon. Doc and Junior were laying new tarpaper on the roof of the tool shed. Lee stood on the ground, beneath the ladder.

"Boys, are you working hard or hardly working?" Curtis asked when he pulled up.

"I'm a working hard," Doc yelled. "I can't speak for these other'uns."

"You wouldn't help a man out this evening?" Curtis asked.

"I reckon we might," Doc said.

Lee steadied his weight against the ladder as Doc and Junior started down, Doc carrying what was left of the roll of tarpaper, Junior bringing the bucket of nails and the hammers. They stowed the tools and tarpaper in the shed. They brought extra hoes and climbed in the truck with Curtis, Lee sitting in the middle near the shift where he had to move his legs every time Curtis changed gears.

"It's a hot'un," Curtis said. "Day like this I wish I was back in the mines."

"Why ain't you?" Lee asked, feeling the point of Doc's elbow in his side as soon as he spoke.

Curtis rolled his shoulders and stared out his window. He wiped his hand across his mouth, mumbled something beneath his fingers, then he spat out the window. "Hotter than a firecracker," he said.

Curtis' piece of bottom land was less than fifty feet wide but it hugged the creek bank for over a hundred yards. Half had been planted in corn, the stalks standing bare and dry now. A small pumpkin patch grew at one end, the pumpkins just beginning to ripen.

"Here we are, boys," Curtis said, stopping the truck. "You all pile out. I need to go to the house for a minute."

Doc and Junior and Lee waved to Donnie as they strolled into the field. Donnie stood at the end of the corn patch. He had chopped two full rows and raked the stalks into a heap at the garden's end. He rested on his hoe, staring at the ground and smiling. He beckoned to Lee, and Lee ran to where he stood. A tortoise was poised at Donnie's feet, its head pointed toward the road, motionless as stone. Lee squatted. He tipped its head with a piece of straw and it pulled quickly back into its shell. Donnie picked it up and carried it across the field, setting it gently at the edge.

They started at opposite corners of the field, working toward the center. Lee's hoe was too long for him to handle easily, but he slashed wildly and managed to go nearly half as fast as the older boys. No one spoke to him about the job he was doing, though when they were finishing, Donnie went over Lee's rows and cleaned up what he had missed. They cleared the field in less than an hour, then raked the stalks into even piles and sat down in the middle of the stubbled field to rest.

"I heard fire got out again," Junior said, "at Decoy."

"I heard somebody let it out," Donnie said.

"People burn their brush too early in the day," Doc said.

"I don't mean by accident," Donnie said. "I heard somebody let it out on purpose."

"What for?" Lee asked.

"Meanness," Doc answered.

"Reckon it's safe to burn this here?" Donnie asked.

"It's past the curfew," Doc said.

The slam of a door echoed across the field, and they all looked up at the same time, toward Curtis' house on the easternmost hillside. Curtis was ambling down the pathway, side to side, arms askance, like a sailor on a rolling boat. Doc and Junior both snickered then hushed at Donnie's silence. Lee stared. Curtis weaved into the bottom, his head abob like a strutting rooster's.

"What kind a job'je do?" he yelled.

The boys all rose slowly to their feet, though none of them spoke. Doc had filled his lip with snuff, his mouth drawn halfway between a smile and a frown. Junior stood with his shoulders hunched, his hands in his pockets. Lee copied him. Donnie stared at the creek, his back to his father's approach.

"What kind a job'je do?" he yelled again when he was a bit closer. He stumbled, but managed not to fall. Then he cursed the dirt row that had tripped him.

"You boys are awful good to help me," he said when he stood among them, "awful good to help me out." His sour breath hung thickly in the air.

Doc grinned around his lump of snuff and spat a gob into the dirt. "Ah," he said, "we're glad to do it."

Curtis smiled broadly. "You boys are just like my own young'uns," he said. "I make no difference between you."

"We was debating whether to risk burning this off," Doc said.

Curtis looked around at the newly cleared field. He pulled a cigar from his shirt pocket and stuck it between his teeth. "Why not?" he asked.

"It's still windy," Donnie said, turning for the first time to face his father.

"Ah," Curtis said. "We'll watch it." He snapped open a shiny metal lighter and lit his cigar, then he carried the open flame to the nearest brush pile, knelt and lit it. He picked up a hoe and plunged the blade into the fire, pulling out a chunk of flame to splash into another pile of rubbish. He went from pile to pile throughout the field, until they were all ablaze. Donnie and Doc and Junior and Lee stood in a circle around the burning brush, their hoes shouldered like rifles.

A breeze ruffled the light scatter of leaves on the willows by the creek. Lee smelled the silt stirring in the low water. He smelled the rotten grasses and corn stalks, their odor sweet as they burned.

Later, when the fire had died and the field was bare and black, Curtis patted the boys on the back, hitched up his pants and headed for the house. Donnie offered the other boys a ride home, and they all crowded into Curtis' pickup. Donnie gunned the engine when they started and swerved the old truck toward the side of the road where he had laid the terrapin. After that, he drove slowly and steadily and didn't speak.

For a long while that evening, Lee sat with his mother on the porch. He lay next to her in the glider while she peeled and quartered Winesap apples and dropped them into a big wooden bowl, the peels curling off to the side into a paper grocery sack. Doc and Junior stood in the front yard, casting their rod and reels at the row of chrysanthemums planted along the driveway.

Lee was dozing when he heard his father's truck. He jumped up and ran off the porch, meeting his father as he got out of the cab. He took his father's lunch box and hard hat and walked along behind him. His father stopped to sit on the porch steps and undo his coal blackened boots and take off his shirt and socks. His clothes were black with coal dust. His nose was smudged, and there were circles of dust underneath his eyes.

He'd sat there barely five minutes before they heard the mufflerless roar of Curtis' pickup plowing up the holler. Lee's father sighed, slipped on his boots and began to snug the laces. His mother continued to pare apples and didn't look up when the truck pulled in. Doc and Junior reeled in their lines and stood quietly by the driveway.

Donnie was at the wheel. His left cheek was bruised, the lid of his left eye slightly swollen. "Howdy," he said.

Lee's father rose slowly to his feet and smiled. "Have you come to supper?"

"No," Donnie said, staring at the center of the truck's steering wheel.

"Is something wrong?"

"Mommy was wondering if you could come up to the house," Donnie said.

"Is something wrong with Curtis?"

Donnie didn't answer for a moment. He stared hard at the steering wheel. "Daddy's took a spell," he said, finally.

"I'll be right along," Lee's father said.

Donnie nodded. He backed the truck out of the driveway and sat, idling, by the side of the road. When Lee's father went to get in his own truck, Lee ran around to the passenger side and started to pull the door open.

Lee's mother called to them. "Lee don't need to go," she said. His father nodded and told him to stay home. "You tell Curtis to straighten hisself out," she continued, "Ain't no excuse for such as him."

"Curt does the best he can," Lee's father said, then he got in the truck.

In a little while, Lee's mother rose and went into the house. His brothers wandered off, seeking new targets for their casting. Lee walked slowly down the driveway. He looked back once to see that no one was watching, then began to run along the road toward his uncle's house. It was less than a mile's distance, and Lee was there before the evening shade had fully settled in.

The two pickups were parked next to the coal pile. The door of his father's truck was slightly ajar, and the interior light was on. Lee pulled the door open and slammed it shut, and the light went off.

He climbed the slope to the house. The front yard was steep and rocky and cluttered with automobile parts and broken tools and half-rotten boards filled with bent, rusted nails. As he came into the back yard, he heard the blast and saw the flash of a shotgun, and then the limb of a poplar burst and fell to the ground in a rain of sticks and leaves.

Curtis stood within the shower of debris, opening the breech of the single barrel shotgun to pop out the spent shell and load in a fresh one. Lee's father stood just behind Curtis, his hands in his pockets, shoulders slumped, staring tiredly at the shot tree. The two had the same features, but Curtis looked old and crooked, his face and body sagging with extra flesh while Lee's father was lean and firm.

Curtis' wife, Connie, stood at the back door, her arms wrapped around her, a cigarette in her mouth, the smoke curling up around the high pile of her blond hair. She opened the door a crack and beckoned with a shaky hand. "Lee," she hissed, "Baby, come here." Lee saw that she was crying, the cigarette trembling in her mouth.

Donnie stood at the edge of the yard, his arms crossed tightly on his chest as he glared at his father.

Curtis leaned on the edge of a cable spool he'd upended

for a table. He drank from a large plastic cup, then he shouldered the shotgun and aimed it jerkily at a garbage bag filled with cans. He shot and stumbled backward, and the garbage bag blew apart, cans and bits of plastic flying across the yard.

Lee's father caught Curtis as he fell. "Careful, old buddy," he said. He laughed and slapped Curtis on the back with one hand and gripped the barrel of the shotgun with the other.

Curtis stared dumbly for a moment, then he grinned. He laughed and leaned his face close to Lee's father's and patted his jaw. "Let go of my gun," he said.

"Now, no," Lee's father said, "you need to put it up." He tried to pull the shotgun away, but Curtis held tightly to it.

"I ain't done shooting," Curtis said and wrenched the gun from his brother's grasp. He turned, pulling the trigger before he'd even raised the gun to his shoulder. A yellow squash exploded, scattering mush and bits of shell across the yard just as the shotgun leapt from Curtis' hands and Curtis fell.

Lee's father retrieved the shotgun. He breeched it, popped out the spent shell and carried the weapon across the yard. "Put this up somewhere," he said, handing the gun to Connie. Connie's hands shook as she took the gun. She slumped under its weight.

Curtis lay on his back under the poplar. He moaned when Lee's father hauled him to his feet.

"Let's go see about some supper," Lee's father suggested.

Curtis went down on one knee and Lee's father motioned for Donnie to come help. Donnie moved hesitantly to take Curtis' arm, but when Curtis saw his face he shrugged him off. "Let me alone," he said. Then he and Lee's father continued toward the house, and Donnie walked off into the woods.

"You still working in them old mines?" Curtis asked.

"I still am," Lee's father replied.

"You need to get out of them old mines," Curtis said.

"I'll quit tomorrow."

"It's a fix," Curtis said.

They walked a few steps more, then Curtis went down again. Lee's father rested for a minute, then he pulled his brother to his feet and started him walking again.

"You'll make out," Curtis said. "I'll help you."

The woods behind Curtis' house had been missed by the summer fires, though the trees were dry and the ground covered with brittle leaves and pine needles. When Lee found Donnie he was seated on the trunk of a large sycamore that had uprooted and fallen into a cluster of beech trees, taking a few of the younger, smaller trees down with it. Lee stopped as soon as he saw him and squatted behind a patch of laurel.

It seemed to Lee that Donnie sat on the trunk for a long while, his hands clasped in his lap, rocking slightly back and forth. After a while he rose and climbed a little higher on the hill. He knelt by a thicket of dead blackberry briars, his head bent, his face pale and bruised and scowling.

Lee watched quietly as Donnie took Curtis' lighter from his pocket and clicked open the lid. He thought that Donnie was about to spark the lighter, but Donnie just stared at it for a long while then closed the lid and slipped it back into his pocket. Eventually, Donnie rose and walked deeper into the hills.

Lee followed at a distance, moving as slowly and quietly as he could through the tangles of dead, dry brush.

FIRST OF THE MONTH

I despise the first of the month. You can't get on the road for the welfare cases. I see Dougie Johnston at the mouth of Brushy Creek. I try to just cruise on by, like I don't see him standing there in his black turtleneck sweater and oversize camouflage pants and chewed up Reds cap stuck backwards on his head that he found in the middle of the road somewhere.

He stares me down, not even holding his thumb out, just standing there, pitiful, waiting. I go on by for a ways, make it almost, but then I look in the rear view mirror and my foot hits the brake in spite of what I want, and he comes running up to the pickup and hops in the cab like my long lost pal.

"I didn't think you seen me for a minute," he says. "I sure do appreciate you stopping."

"Yeah, man," I say. "No problem."

"Where you headed?" he asks.

"County market."

"That's lucky for me."

He sits crouched up, hands on his knees, looking straight ahead. He doesn't move the whole ride. But he talks. That's how he gets around you. "Your wife all right?" he asks.

"Why wouldn't she be all right?" I snap. "There ain't been nothing in the paper about her not being all right, not that I know of."

"I reckon," Dougie says.

I don't speak again for a while. I'm remembering Roberta when we were first married. I'm remembering the second-hand trailer we lived in the first five years, how we went without water when the pipes froze, without electricity when I was out of work. I'm thinking how what got us through was having to pull together so hard just to scrape by. I'm thinking about us now, how we come and go, say "hello" and "thank you" and "excuse me" to each other like strangers.

We ride up Polk Mountain, lay over for a loaded down Mack we meet in a switchback curve. The driver pulls his horn. I recognize the name "Black Cat" painted on the truck's door, wave my arm out my window, and yell, "Hey, Patton."

Near the mountaintop I pull off to view the strip site. This is one of John Winfrey's biggest operations. Half the mountain, two thousand acres, has been honed down. I sit for a while and watch the D-9 dozers and backhoes gouging up coal, the endloaders scooping it into the Mack trucks. The smell of diesel fuel rises on a little breeze, and I can feel the rumble of heavy equipment right in my chest.

"Sure is something," Dougie says.

For a second I'd forgot he was in the truck with me. I don't answer, just put her in gear and head on down the mountain.

We drive through Palestine, row on row of tiny box-frame houses propped on stilts on the hillside above the old C&O

railway spur. Each one is like the other, two windows to a side, no porch, rusty metal stovepipes sticking through gray tarpaper roofs. A few of the houses that are still yet lived in have been kept up, but most of them are falling in on themselves. There's talk of opening up a section of the old deep mine, restoring the company commissary and a few of the old houses and running tours through. I'd like to get in on that.

We bypass the county seat and head out on Highway 1 to the County Market. The parking lot is filled with rolling wrecks, just bits and pieces of cars, not one of them whole. I find a space next to the war monument, a World War II Howitzer, shut her off and start to climb out, but before I do old Dougie says reckon I couldn't let him have a dollar or two.

It ain't like I didn't expect it, but even so it pisses me off. I grew up with this boy. I know his people. My daddy and his daddy both worked in the mines. My daddy stove his leg up under a shuttle car. His daddy claimed black lung. Claimed it. I ain't saying a lot of folks don't deserve them benefits. I ain't saying that at all. But they's some that don't. Some that cheat and lie. I don't mind a feller getting what's coming to him. And I don't mind helping a feller out. It ain't that at all. But when my daddy couldn't hump no more, he didn't stick out his thumb for a free ride. He borrowed on the homeplace, leased some machinery, and put us boys to work.

We had fifty acres in the head of Bear Creek, a good lot of timber and a four foot seam of coal just under the ridge. We hauled out the timber on twenty-five acres, then we stripped it. Daddy said that busted leg was the best thing that ever

67

happened to him, made him start relying on himself instead of other people. I think about that when Dougie Johnston asks me couldn't I let him have a dollar or two. I think, "By God, I never took Dougie Johnston to raise." And I say it too.

"By God, Dougie, I ain't took you to raise."

Dougie just nods and slides out of the cab. "We thank you for the ride," he says. I feel a little bit bad then, so I pull a couple of ones from my billfold and start to hand them over. He doesn't even blink, just reaches his hand to take them, and I realize I'm not sticking up for what I believe. So I pull the bills back and stick them in my shirt pocket. I know how that must look, but a man's got to stick up for what he believes.

Alicia Wingate's list is filled with last minute party items—5 pounds of butterfly shrimp, 5 jars of smoked herring in sour cream, 4 jars of black olives/pitted, 5 jars of marinated artichoke hearts, 3 pounds of ripe lemons. The word "ripe" is underlined. It's a testament to progress that a grocery in this part of the state would stock such items. Ten years ago it would have been unheard of. Strides have been made.

Now and again I catch sight of old Dougie Johnston as I make my way through the aisles. I see him pilfering through the rolls of unsliced bologna, squeezing the loaves of day old light bread, sniffing the packs of discount chicken wings. He's among his own today. The store's full of cases just like him—skinny, scraggly haired men and obese women trailing screaming kids; grandmaws and grandpaws doddering along behind, toothless, bent over, broken down, uneasy so far from the head of the holler. You can always tell when the welfare checks have come out.

One old codger pops up in my face as I'm ordering my butterfly shrimp.

"Use a good knife, buddy?" he asks. He has two used pocket knives in the palm of his hand. They look like something hammered together in a sweat shop in Pakistan. The grips are plastic. The blades are black with tarnish. "Give you a good deal," he says.

"No, I got a good knife," I answer and turn away to watch the lady weigh out my shrimp.

"Well," he says, "I reckon if a man's got a good knife, he don't need another'un." He doesn't go away though. He stands next to me and stares at that iced shrimp piling up on the scales. "Them are shore big crawdads," he says. I glance over to see if he's joking. I can't tell, and the glance is all he needs to start in. "I recollect the feller went swimming in a creek full of crawdads," he says. He pauses. His eyes go blank for a second. He's trying to tell a joke, but he's lost the thread of it.

I take a good look at him while he's off trying to find his thoughts. I've never seen such a beat-up looking face. The skin is peppered with flecks of coal dust. The lines in it could be hundreds of years old, but I take him to be about sixty. He has big hands for a little man. They're callused all over, not just the palms. The fingers, the thumbs, and the heels are all covered with thick, dead horns of skin. His nails are long and broken. They are dirty and blackened with injury. His eyes lose some of their blankness while I stare at him.

"That time I never even heard no noise," he says, almost in a whisper, "just felt all the air blow out of the hole." Then he blinks, and his eyes are all clear. "Use a good knife?" he asks.

"No," I say and take my shrimp and get away. I don't know what old hurt was coming back on him. I don't need to know. Every face in this store has got some old hurt ready to flare up.

I'm not surprised when Dougie Johnston hails me in the parking lot and asks if I'm heading back toward the county seat. I lie and say I'm not.

I've hauled for John Wingate for ten years. I drive my own truck, mine and the bank's. Roberta and I are looking to build on Millionaire's Ridge. We're not millionaires, but we've done all right. We've got a twenty-foot pontoon on Laurel Lake. She drives a Camry. I've got this new Dodge Ram. All this comes from work.

When the coal run out on that first twenty-five acres, I talked Daddy into mining the other half. He was reluctant. "What's the use of being land poor?" I asked him. He'd grown up in them hills, he said. Hated to see it all go. But he finally saw the profit. We were still hauling coal out of there when he died.

Little brother and I got joint ownership of the land. I sold my share of the equipment to him and started trucking, but I've got a scheme to develop that property. A couple of tracts have been leveled enough for a trailer park or a shopping plaza. All I need is a little working capital. Little brother and me are both mortgaged to the hilt. Red ink goes with the territory.

Millionaire's Ridge is a prime example of what can be

done with reclamation. It rises 2,000 feet above sea level, even with being stripped. The highway going up was once an access road. The house lots are in what was once a mining pit. There's a highwall at the north end that keeps the wind down. The slag has been dozed over and fill dirt brought in and fescue planted. There's a buttress built all around the ridge to keep the whole thing from sliding off. And the view is tremendous. You can look down on the center of town, on the other ridges that have been stripped and reclaimed, made even and level and grassy. There's the beginning of a horse trail that goes for twenty miles across the county and links up with seven different strip sites. There's room for pasture land now, or golf courses, or trailer parks.

Roberta's Camry is parked in the Wingate's driveway, behind Alicia's 321 BMW and in front of a Nissan 300Z and a new Cadillac El Dorado. I park my pickup on the shoulder of the road.

I don't know the girl who answers the door. She's about eighteen, dressed in cutoff jeans, a tie-dyed tee shirt, and a pair of bright red Chuck Taylor high top sneakers. She has blonde hair done up in corn rows. She backs out of the doorway and yells over her shoulder. "Alicia, there's a guy here…." I push on through before she has a chance to confirm my admittance. I lug the groceries down the hall to the kitchen.

Alicia Wingate and Roberta are seated at the kitchen table. I almost drop the beer when I see Alicia's face. I almost say, "My God, what happened to you?" Both her eyes are blacked. Her nose is bandaged and swollen. I almost say, "What'd you tangle with?" But before I do, I remember

Roberta saying something about plastic surgery, and I just nod. But my face has given me away. Alicia's hand flutters up to cover her nose. Roberta glares.

John comes in from the patio to rescue the moment. "Rick," he says, "this is Ann Marie Morehead." He turns to the girl who wasn't sure I should be in the house. "Ann Marie is here with the Christian Appalachian Project." Then he puts his hand on my arm and says, "Ann Marie, this is Rick Baker, one of my best men." Ann Marie cocks her head back, goes "ah" to herself, like now she understands, and reaches out her hand. I wipe mine on my pants before I shake.

I can feel Roberta watching me. I don't want to mess up again and make us look bad. I'm relieved when John steers me out to the patio. I don't know either of the guys out there, but they have the look of capital about them. The young guy, Steve Thompson, is the son of one of John's old buddies who John is teaching the coal business. I pair him with the Nissan.

The other guy, Louis Kellum, is dressed like a rich cowboy, leather sports coat and a pair of thousand dollar ostrich skin boots. He has something like a cowboy accent, like I think one would be, but it's a little too slick. I figure he drives the Cad.

We stand around for a while and talk. Steve Thompson seems all right. He and John talk golf. When John mentions how nice it'd be to have a course in the county someday, a real course, not some par three, I take the opportunity to mention how ripe this county is for development. "All kinds of possibilities," I say. Louis Kellum snorts and looks off across the ridge tops.

"I've been thinking about some development of my own," I say, and I outline my plans for a trailer park. John hears me out. Steve Thompson looks interested, but Louis Kellum keeps his back turned, keeps staring across the ridges.

"Minimum investment, low maintenance and good returns over the long term," I say, looking directly at Steve Thompson.

John pats me on the back before I finish and says, "How about checking on the refreshments."

In the kitchen the ladies are slicing lemons into pitchers of ice water and artificial sweetener. Ann Marie is telling about her social service work. She has a way of turning everything she says into a question.

"It's worse than you imagine?" she says. "A dozen people sometimes in a rusty trailer? Or a shack no bigger than this kitchen?"

Alicia nods.

"Whatever we do, it's just never enough? And in the end they resent us?"

"There's just so much built-in failure to overcome," Alicia says. She sighs a little, brings a tissue to her bandaged nose. "Am I right, Roberta? You're from here. You've had to overcome your background."

"Oh yes," Roberta says, then covers her mouth with her fingers.

"What do you think, Rick?" Alicia asks. "Is Ann Marie wasting her time?"

I stare at Roberta for a moment. Her cheeks have been shaded to points, her hair trimmed short of her collar and

73

styled into a silver stranded helmet, like Alicia's. Her eyebrows are plucked thin and drawn into arches. She smiles like her jaw is broken.

"Welfare kills the gumption in people," I say, without really thinking, "so does your volunteer programs." The room gets quiet. I pause to consider what I've said, try to remember who I'm talking to. The CAP girl sits forward in her chair, chewing a thumbnail, frowning. I realize my mistake. "Why, honey," I say, "you're not wasting your time. Long as you feel good about what you're doing."

They all scowl. I shuffle my feet a little. "Don't pay no attention to me," I say. I take a full pitcher of lemonade and and a few glasses then head for the outdoors.

"Incentives," John is saying. "If we're going to attract new industry to this area, we need to offer incentives."

"Amen to that," I say.

"Incentives in the form of tax breaks. Of cost reduction. We've got to offer recreational facilities and better schools. We've got to improve our infrastructure. We've got to give corporate America a reason to locate here."

The women come out to join us. Alicia sets extra glasses on the patio table and goes to stand next to John. Roberta stays clear of me. When she glances in my direction, there's nothing in her eyes I know how to read.

I once heard that love is just hormones. People fall in love for the high and fall out of love when the high wears off. That's the reason so many marriages fail in the first two years. The high wears off.

I don't know about Roberta and me. We've been together

for fifteen years, and I can't say at this moment whether I'm in or out of love with her.

Roberta is smiling her broken-jawed smile. She's not a homely woman, but there's something about the way she stands, with her shoulders slightly stooped, that next to Alicia Wingate makes her look not as good. It may be the way I look at her. It may be the way I look next to John Wingate. I feel bad. When I reach for the pitcher of lemonade, I'm just clumsy enough to tip it over. It shatters against the deck, a splatter of fine crystal, lemon slices, and ice cubes.

The back of my neck gets hot. I kneel to pick up the pieces of glass. Roberta brings a towel from the kitchen to help mop up. I watch her face as we work. I wish she'd look at me.

Alicia brings a fresh pitcher. Nobody mentions my mishap, and after a while I feel like I'm among friends again.

Roberta and I stand together for a minute, watching John and Alicia slow dance across the deck. John sings softly in Alicia's ear, and Alicia giggles in a way I would've never thought she could. Steve Thompson and the CAP girl whisper to each other and stare off over the ridge tops, holding hands. Louis Kellum hangs on the rail, keeping to himself.

The CAP girl wanders back into the house, then Roberta makes her getaway. When Kellum drains his glass and goes inside, I corner Steve Thompson. I tell jokes and get him to laugh. I get him to tell jokes, and I laugh. I agree with his politics. I admire his car. I cross over to his religion. Then I get down to business. Within half an hour we have a verbal commitment to a written commitment to an agreement that will be mutually beneficial to both of us, but mostly to me. We raise our glasses of lemonade and drink to prosperity.

The CAP girl returns. John and Alicia are still dancing, so I excuse myself and head inside. When I enter the kitchen, I hear Roberta's muffled voice mingled with Kellum's snaky cowboy drawl. Kellum has his arms around Roberta, and Roberta is pushing him away. I can't tell if she's laughing or crying.

Kellum is already on the floor by the time I feel my fist smash into his face. I've not punched anyone since I was in the army. I feel none of the wild release of adrenaline. The flash of anger that set me off becomes a steady ache inside my gut.

The next thing I know the party has moved indoors, and I'm the center of attention. For some reason I think about the old codger in the County Market, about the years he must've spent in the mines to get that face of his, about the busted joints and cracked bones he must've suffered and about the memory of pain that's all he's left with for all his work.

I help Kellum to his feet, offer him a handkerchief for his busted nose, dust him off. He pushes me away and stalks out of the kitchen. I see lost opportunity on Steve Thompson's face. When I look at John, his face gets hard, and for a minute I feel like I'm on the job and he's about to come down on me.

I say my apologies as much as I can. I say I'm sorry about the pitcher I broke. I say I'm sorry about the mess in the kitchen. I tell Steve Thompson we'll have to talk business sometime. I tell John Wingate I'll see him Monday. I say to Alicia, "Thank you for having us." I say to the CAP girl, "It's been nice to meet you." I say, "I'm sorry we have to go now."

We leave Roberta's Camry blocked by all that rolling money and climb into the pickup. Roberta's quiet. I look at her, and I think, "Lord, what just happened?"

Before we even get close to home, I see a figure on the roadside. Who else but Dougie Johnson? He's lugging a sack full of groceries back to Brushy Creek. He steps off the road when he sees us coming. I tap the brakes.

I see Roberta tense as Dougie climbs into the cab. He smiles at both of us, nods to Roberta, and settles in next to the door, keeping a polite distance.

Right off Dougie asks Roberta how her dad has been. She tells him about his bursitis, and Dougie says how he reckons he ought to stop by and visit. Roberta asks Dougie how his mom and dad are, and Dougie says, "Oh, about the same." By the time we pass through Palestine, Roberta has relaxed a little. She and Dougie talk family all the way up Polk Mountain.

I pull over when we get to the mouth of Brushy Creek. Roberta manages a weak smile as Dougie gets out of the cab. "Thank you for the ride," he says, and for a second I think he's going to put the touch on me, but he just tips the brim of his cap at Roberta and heads up the holler with his sack full of groceries. I think about going after him, maybe slipping him a few dollars. It would help him out. It would make me feel better.

I shut off the truck when Roberta says, "Come on, let's go." I can feel her staring at me, but I just sit there, thinking things over. She settles in on her side of the cab to do her own thinking. It gets dark. We watch the moon come up over Auglin Mountain. The outfit that stripped it has yet to do any reclamation. The bare knobs of rock shine white as bone in the full moon's light. I hear a dragline start up on a strip job five miles away. I think about all the money to be made in this world. I wonder if I'll have a job on Monday or a wife.

EMINENT DOMAIN

As Herbert Ray got out of his car he heard the steady clatter of his father's meal grinder. He stood for a moment and watched the tin roof of the work shed shiver. His father liked to say he'd invented the contraption. It had come whole from a Sears Roebuck catalogue in the late thirties, but almost every piece on it had been maintained through retooling.

After a moment the grinder sputtered to a stop, and his father came from the shed, carrying a paper sack. He opened it and poured a little of the newly ground meal into Herbert Ray's hand. Herbert Ray made a fist around the smooth meal and raised his hand to let it trickle through his fingers and back into the sack. Then the two of them walked side by side to the house, Herbert Ray lengthening his stride just a little to keep pace with his father's long legged gait.

With the grinder shut off, Herbert Ray could hear the faint rumble of endloaders and rock trucks and D-9 dozers. He could hear the dynamite blasts, like rolling thunder from a coming storm, could almost feel the ground tremble through the soles of his boots.

Herbert Ray's youngest son, Coy, sat on the bottom step of the porch, a partially dismantled lawnmower motor at his feet.

"How's she going," Herbert Ray asked.

Coy raised his hand, a fuel gasket pinched between his thumb and forefinger. "Here's some of the problem," he said. "But not all."

"Did you do any work today?" Herbert Ray asked.

"I never got started," Coy replied.

"When's your brother coming in?" Herbert Ray asked. Coy shrugged.

"Said they'd be here for supper," a voice called from the house. Herbert Ray looked up to see his wife, Betty, peering through the screen door. "I made a baked ham and fried sweet potatoes and a pot of shucky beans," she said, "and fried apples and two skillets of cornbread and blackberry dumplings."

Herbert Ray opened his lunch bucket and tossed a few crusts of light bread into the yard. A pair of blue jays dove from a nearby poplar and plucked them up at once. "He'll want to go to the homeplace," he said, "and look for that old grave site again."

"I'm not going," Coy said. "We spend a whole day tramping through the hills and never find a thing."

"You don't go just to find something," Herbert Ray said.

"I lost all of today," Coy said. "I need to work tomorrow."

They stopped talking as the construction noise, which had quieted down some toward the end of the work day, finally ceased altogether. Within a few minutes the sound of automobile engines could be heard, at first distantly then nearer and nearer. The sound grew until the cars and pick-up trucks began to roar by in a swirl of dust and skipping gravel.

Some of the men in the passing vehicles waved their hands and blew their horns. Herbert Ray, recognizing the dust and sweat-grimed faces of men he had worked with over the years, raised his hand to wave back.

When all the cars and trucks had passed, the ripple of the nearby creek became clear, then the croaking of frogs, the chirrup of crickets, and the squeak of bats flocking into the dusky sky.

"I doubt Kenneth being here in time for supper," Herbert Ray said.

At just after ten that night Herbert Ray's oldest son, Kenneth, arrived with his wife, Vivian. Coy went outside to help his brother with the suitcases. Betty went out to take Vivian's arm and help her into the house.

"Now, Betty, I can manage fine," Vivian said, her ruffled maternity blouse stretching tight across her abdomen as she walked.

When all the bags and bundles were inside Coy, Kenneth, Vivian, and Herbert Ray sat at the kitchen table.

Betty began taking the still warm bowls of food from the oven.

Vivian reached her hand to her father-in-law. "Herbert Ray," she said, "how are you?"

"Fine," Herbert Ray said. Then he asked how their trip had been, and Vivian said, "Fine."

"They're making progress on that new road," Kenneth said.

"It's moving along," Herbert Ray said. "Lots of men working on it."

"They're still hiring," Coy said. He paused and glanced at his father. "I've put in an application."

"Well," Herbert Ray said, "that's news."

Kenneth stared silently at Coy for a moment, then he turned to Herbert Ray. "Have you come to terms with the state?"

"We'll take what they offer us," Herbert Ray replied. Kenneth scooted his chair forward to allow his mother to pass behind him with a full skillet of cornbread and a bowl of fried sweet potatoes. She set the food on the table and went back to the stove. She brought the baked ham, the pot of shucky beans, and dish of fried apples. She set out plates, glasses, knives, forks, and spoons.

"We might move into that trailer park on Brushy Creek," Coy said. "They have a satellite dish we can hook onto."

Kenneth and Vivian began to fill their plates, neither speaking again until they'd finished eating.

"Where's Papaw Whitt?" Vivian asked. "Is he all right?"

"Nothing wrong with him," Betty replied. "He fairs better than any of us. He's just gone to bed already."

"I need to ask him some more things," Kenneth said. He opened a portfolio he'd brought to the table. He unfolded a large, heavy piece of paper. A carefully sketched genealogy of the Palmer family filled the entire sheet, extending from the blank to be filled by Kenneth and Vivian's first child to Kenneth's half-Cherokee maternal great-great-great-grandmother, Bertha Horton, who was born in the summer of 1789 and died in the spring of 1850. "I need to know Alice Thacker's maiden name, and I still need to know when Grant Collins was born and died."

"We could try to find that old grave site again," Herbert Ray said.

"I had that in mind," Kenneth said.

"I've got some work lined up," Coy said. "I've got three yards to mow that I didn't get to today."

They were all silent for a moment, then Herbert Ray said, "You ought to go with us."

"All right," Coy said, and for the rest of the evening they talked about family and neighbors and friends—about who was ailing and who was well, about who had died and who had given birth.

At first light the next morning Herbert Ray and Whitt went to the mill shed. They sat for a while on two stacks of milk crates next to the workbench, warming themselves with coffee and listening to the early morning frenzy of bird song.

When they felt themselves fully awake, Herbert Ray hefted the sack of shelled corn Tom Lovis had brought to be ground into feed and set it on a table level with the hopper. Whitt changed the fine burrs that he used for table meal for the coarse ones he used for feed, then he pulled the rope on the 5 hp motor. A few particles of crushed corn spat into the trough as the motor caught. When the pulleys were turning at speed, Herbert Ray poured some of Tom's corn into the hopper. Whitt held his hand before the flow of cracked and crushed corn as it spilled into the trough. He adjusted the burrs as Herbert Ray poured more corn into the hopper, then they both sat back to watch the grinder run.

"People don't bring much corn to be ground anymore," Whitt said, his voice raised to be heard over the grinder.

"They all buy it in the store now," Herbert Ray replied.

"I'm grateful for just enough to keep busy," Whitt said,

"and to keep my grinder running." He rose to pour more corn into the hopper. He ran his hand through the ground feed in the trough. "I wish I had some livestock to tend," he said. "I wish I had a little jenny that was broke to harness, so I could go around and plow up people's gardens every spring."

"Everybody's got tillers, now," Herbert Ray said. He took out his pocketknife, opened the main blade, and tested the edge against the fine hairs on the back of his wrist. "I reckon Coy's going to hire out to work on the new road."

"That Coy's an awful good hand to work," Whitt said.

"He's awful good with motors and tools," Herbert Ray agreed.

"He'd rather work than eat," Whitt said.

They sat quietly for a while, the steady clatter of the grinder shivering their skin. It took less than an hour for them to grind the five bushels of Tom Lovis' corn. When it was finished they sacked it in burlap bags and stacked it in a corner to itself.

"I wish I had a little jenny so me and Coy could hire out to plow people's fields," Whitt said as they walked to the house for their breakfast.

After the men left that day, Betty and Vivian sat in the glider on the front porch. They reached into a bushel basket of fresh picked green beans, breaking them apart and dropping the full hulls into Betty's five quart canning pot. The discarded bean strings made a nest between them.

"Have you and Kenneth thought of names yet?" Betty asked.

"Levi if it's a boy," Vivian said. "And Claire if it's a girl."

"Those are pretty names," Betty said. "Where do they come from?"

"They're from the genealogy of your-all's family."

Betty was silent for a while. She had a pile of beans in her lap. She concentrated on snapping the ends off, pulling the strings out, and breaking them in two until her lap was empty, then she dusted her dress and reached for another handful.

"They go back pretty far," Vivian said. She worked slower than Betty, sometimes breaking the bean strings and having to dig the pieces out with her nails. "Levi comes from Levi Fuller on your side, and Claire comes from Claire Collins on Herbert Ray's. You don't hear names like those much anymore."

Betty paused, resting her hands over the beans in her lap. "Have you thought to name them after your own people?" she asked.

"My family's not close like yours," Vivian said. Then she stopped breaking beans and stared silently at the porch floor.

Betty patted her daughter-in-law's hand. "I was about seven or eight years old when Levi Fuller passed away," she said, "I remember he was a Hard Shell Baptist, and he testified at the first prayer meeting I ever remember. I know he used to drive ponies in the mines when they used them to haul out coal." She paused to fill her lap with fresh beans. "I don't remember much about Claire Collins. Herbert Ray or Whitt might tell you something."

The dirt road leading from the new Palmer homeplace to the old was so grown up with grass and weeds that there was barely a pair of tire tracks to steer by. Stretches had been almost entirely washed out, and Herbert Ray had to ease the pickup through axle deep ruts and over rocks and around boulders and uprooted trees. He drove as slowly as he could and still keep traction, but even so the truck seemed to bounce more than it rolled.

Whitt had to put his false teeth in his shirt pocket to keep them from clattering inside his mouth, and every time Herbert Ray glanced in the rear view mirror to check on his sons riding in the truck bed, one or both of them would be in the air, going up or coming down.

"I don't remember this road being this bad," Herbert Ray said. His words jarred through his teeth. His back ached.

"Time was, this was a good road," Whitt said.

They drove by the steep hillside that had been a pasture for cattle, but that was now filled with huge chunks of rock and overgrown with briars and scrubby pine trees and kudzu. What was left of the rail fence lay scattered along the boundary it had once held. They didn't know they were in the barnyard at first. Then they saw the barn's roof, collapsed beneath a single huge boulder, its broken rafter beams sticking through the tattered tarpaper like the ribs of a dead animal. Herbert Ray stopped the truck.

"This place has taken a wild turn," Whitt said.

Herbert Ray got out of the truck and walked stiffly across the barnyard, a pair of army surplus binoculars strung around his neck. Whitt and Kenneth and Coy followed.

The old house sat on a small barely level piece of ground

just below the road. It was still whole, though a few more stones had fallen from the chimney, and the roof sagged a little more. The hillside had slipped in back of the house, and a mound of dirt lay piled almost to the windowsill of the back bedroom.

"Not much left of the way it was," Whitt said.

"Looks like I remember it," Coy said.

"You're too young to remember it right," Whitt said. "I can remember when this was a show place." He pointed to the south, down the hillside toward a silt pool. "The creek run by there," he said. "We had apple trees—Winesaps and Granny Smith's." Whitt turned in a circle, his finger outstretched. "Over yonder Daddy had his bee gum. That's where the hog lot was. That was the chicken house. There was the well. That was the smokehouse."

"I could be making money right now," Coy muttered.

Herbert Ray looked at his son. "Someday you'll want to know what's been lost here."

Coy turned away.

"Let's walk up the ridge," Kenneth said.

They crossed the road and stepped over the fallen fence rails and made their way among the boulders and through the tangled brush of the old pasture. Herbert Ray had picked up a heavy stick to help him climb. Coy would stalk ahead a few yards then wait, while Kenneth would linger next to Whitt and listen to his grandfather tell of what the farm had once been.

It wasn't until they reached the mountaintop that they saw the largest area of the strip site, maybe thirty acres square. An entire ridge had been sheared off but for a single fifty feet thick pinnacle. It looked like a gnawed away apple core, naked and bleak with just a clump of undergrown pine trees left to cling to the very top.

At one end of the strip site was a pond filled with silt, at the other was an access road where the coal trucks and heavy machinery had rolled in and out. The site had grown over some with weeds and a few scraggly saplings, but they could still see the tracks of bulldozers and endloaders.

Herbert Ray raised his binoculars and looked west into the valley they'd driven out of. "I can make out our house," he said. He turned his body, sweeping the glasses across the valley. "That crew don't never let up," he said, pointing the binoculars at the road construction a few miles across the valley.

He watched an endloader fill a massive rock truck with boulders, a bulldozer maneuver itself deftly around a high-wall. He was surprised at how close the glasses brought the machinery and how clearly he could see the operators. He saw the cloud of a dynamite blast and braced himself for the thunder to follow.

"Think them graves are still there?" Kenneth asked.

"I need to study," Whitt said. "Them graves was dug and filled long before I was born." He stared intently into the valley for a few minutes then looked along the ridge line. "Where have we not looked?" he asked, speaking out loud to himself. "I believe," he said, pointing his finger toward the north, "if we was to walk over toward the head of Branham's Branch, where it's not been stripped, and follow along that ridge...." He paused. "I remember there was supposed to have been a hazelnut tree, and at one time they'd been a meeting stand."

"None of that's likely to be there now," Herbert Ray said.

"This way." Whitt strode along the leveled ridge, and by the time the others began to follow he had entered the ragged tree line. He walked for three quarters of an hour, the others following the crash of his footsteps and the frequent glimpses of his checkered shirt as he emerged from the tangled brush.

"There's a trail here," Whitt called back at one point.

"Let's rest," Herbert Ray said. "I'm give out."

"There's a hazelnut tree," Kenneth shouted.

"That's just a birch," Herbert Ray said.

Kenneth went ahead to where Whitt knelt before a flat gray stone. Coy stood for a moment next to his father, then he too went forward. "What have you found?" he asked.

"I don't know," Whitt said.

"It's a headstone," Kenneth said.

"I don't know," Whitt repeated.

"It's a headstone." Kenneth smiled as he ran his fingers over the stone's featureless surface. "All the carvings wore off, but it's a headstone."

For the next half hour they searched the area around the gray stone. When Kenneth found a pair of depressions in the earth, he said that they were sunken graves, but Whitt said they were sinkholes from an old drift mine. When Kenneth found a rotten plank he said it might be from the meeting stand. Whitt said it was timber from the mine.

"How long we going to be at this?" Coy asked.

"Let's look a little longer," Kenneth said.

"I'll do good to get back to the truck," Herbert Ray said.

"Here's the mouth of the mine," Whitt said. He pointed to a hole in the side of the hill twenty feet below where

89

they'd found the stone and the rotted timber. It was so over-grown with vines and weeds and so filled with dirt and rocks that it looked more like a natural cave than a mine.

Kenneth came and stood before the mine entrance, study-ing it for several moments, then he walked away and settled quietly on a boulder. Coy and Herbert Ray looked at the mine, then they too found places to sit, and after a quarter of an hour of silence and rest they all started back.

Vivian sat at the kitchen table, watching Betty pour the freshly cooked green beans into quart jars, then twist the lids on tightly so they would seal. The jars rattled a little with the distant boom of dynamite blasts.

"You and Kenneth take a few jars of these with you," Betty said. "I don't guess we'll keep a garden next year."

"You'll miss that."

Betty dumped a bowl of uncooked beans into the pot and ran fresh water onto them. She covered the pot and set it on the stove and lit the burner. "Would you like a few of my canning jars?" she asked.

"They won't let us grow a garden where we rent," Vivian said.

Betty opened a cabinet door and took out a metal canister. She opened it and took out three smaller ones, each stacked inside the other. "I doubt I'll have room for these," she said. "I want you to take them." She placed the canisters on the table and sat in the chair across from Vivian.

"I guess I'll have the baby before we get back to visit," Vivian said.

"Are you scared?"

"We were both real scared at first. But after a while we got more excited than scared. Kenneth is more scared than I am right now."

"I don't want to meddle, but I'd like to help any I can."

"I appreciate that. I know Kenneth will appreciate it."

"If you want I could come stay with you after the delivery and help you through."

"Are you sure you'll have to move?"

"Herbert Ray seems to be. He don't say much about it, but he acts like he is."

"I hate to see this place gone. I can't imagine your-all's family without this farm. My people are scattered all over the place. Daddy lives in Indiana. Mommy lives in Georgia. I've got a sister somewhere in Florida. I don't know where my brother is. I hate to see you-all break apart."

"We'll stay a family," Betty said, then she rose and went to the stove, lifting the lid from the slowly boiling beans and stirring them with a wooden spoon. "I want you and Kenneth to have my grandmother's old bed frame. If we move into that trailer, we'll have to get a smaller one."

Herbert Ray got up before daylight on the day Kenneth and Vivian were to leave and slipped quietly from the sleeping house. He stood for a while in the yard in the pre-dawn light, the dew moist on his shoes and the cuffs of his pants.

A rooster crowed from a neighboring barnyard. The sky darkened a little as the false dawn faded, and for a little while the stars shone brightly again. He walked across the yard toward the well box, careful of the slight ridges where the water pipes were buried. He ran his hand over the well box, across the impression of Kenneth's six year old feet, wondered if he could chip that out without shattering the cement. Kenneth was twenty-six now. The well box was twenty years old.

The sky lightened, the stars fading altogether. Herbert Ray walked on. He touched the cool walls of his father's work shed. He moved the wooden peg holding the door and looked inside. Even in the dark he knew the shapes of everything the shed held—the hoes, mattocks, and shovels hanging from the walls, the empty paper sacks and burlap bags piled in the corner, the machine lathe on the work bench, the meal grinder in the center of the room. He closed the door, sliding the wooden peg back into place.

He passed by the coal bin, the moist smell of it a dank reminder of the mines. He kicked a chunk of coal, its brittle edges shattering as it rolled from the pile.

He crossed the single lane road and walked over the foot-bridge to the garden, resting for a moment against the limber trunk of a willow. He looked at the corn patch, almost a full acre, at the bean vines trailing up the tall stalks. He thought to gather some green onions and a poke full of leaf lettuce for Kenneth and Vivian; instead he rose and walked a little ways up the hillside that bordered the garden.

He stood and watched the leaves on the trees catch the morning sun. In a little while the house and yard grew bright. The tin roof of his father's work shed gleamed. The garden shone green and moist. The creek sparkled.

He tried to see it all gone and though he knew from experience the false permanence of land, he could not imagine four lanes of asphalt and concrete in place of a house, a yard, a garden. He tried to think of living in a trailer in a trailer park—his whole family packed into a metal box that was ten feet away from another metal box, that was ten feet away from another.... He couldn't see that either.

When he saw Betty come onto the porch of the house, he started back. By the time he reached the yard, the sun was hot, and he could hear the rumble of machinery waking across the valley.

After breakfast Kenneth loaded the suitcases into the car along with the half dozen quart jars of green beans and Betty's canisters. Vivian had almost cried when he suggested they take the bed frame on the next trip, so he and Coy tied it to the roof of the car.

Coy had fixed his lawnmower early in the morning and loaded it into Herbert Ray's truck. As soon as he finished helping Kenneth with the bed frame, he said for them to drive careful and he'd see them next time, then he jumped in the truck and took off.

Whitt came out of the house and patted Vivian on the shoulder and squeezed Kenneth's arm, then he loped across the yard to his shed. The meal grinder clattered to life almost as soon as he closed the door.

Betty and Vivian stood for a long time on the porch, talking and saying good-bye, so Herbert Ray and Kenneth stood by the car and talked.

"I'll see about retaining a lawyer," Kenneth said.

"No use," Herbert Ray replied.

"Don't let them run you over," Kenneth said.

"We'll move aside," Herbert Ray replied.

After they left, Herbert Ray said that he needed to walk

around. Betty sat on the porch, threading raw green beans onto a string. Later she would hang them in the sun to dry. Whitt's meal grinder clattered steadily, drowning out all other noise, though now and then the porch quivered just a little with the ever nearer explosions.

AS A SNARE

Taulbee woke with no feeling in his right arm. He had slept crossways on the couch, halfway on and halfway off, his arm jammed between his body and the floor. When he pushed himself up and the blood began to circulate, he felt like his arm had been run through his grandmother's old wringer washing machine.

Sitting upright for a while took the edge off the prickle of returning blood flow. In a little while all he felt was a tingle on the back of his hand and a slight numbness in his finger-tips. He felt good. His before-the-fact hangover cure of half a Xanax and a single hit of pot had done him right.

The living room was a mess of beer cans, drink glasses, filled ashtrays, spillage of all sorts. Taulbee picked through the nearest ashtray for a roach to smoke; finding none long enough, he lay three small ones in a fresh cigarette paper and rolled them again. He lay back, lit the joint and studied the picture of Jesus hung above the couch.

In the painting the saviour knelt amongst a flock of sheep, his face raised to receive a beam of heavenly light. The halo's 20 watt bulb, concealed within the gold-plated frame, had been burned out for several months.

After his father's death, Taulbee had moved back into the family home. The two bedroom house that had seemed too small when he was growing up now seemed large for his solitary daily living. He'd parceled out some of the furniture and housewares to the closest kin, but he'd kept all of his father's clothing and tools and the family photographs that lined the mantel. For some reason he'd kept the Jesus painting.

Before long the dope eased him into wakefulness. He rubbed the grit from his eyes and rose to the job of cleaning house.

The stereo was still on, the speakers hissing empty air. He remembered zonking out to Dwight Yoakum's 'Hillbilly Highway,' looking up from the floor to watch Sammy Smith perform a drunken clog not very far from his head. He flicked the switch on the stereo. The speakers faded with a pop. Taulbee hoped they weren't blown.

He opened a window, holding it with one hand while he reached for a prop on the nearby shelf with the other. He wedged a heavy book in place and crossed the room to open another window so the air would breeze through.

A tangle of blankets stirred in the corner. A soiled cowboy boot emerged from one end, an uncombed head from the other. "What time is it?" Roe Vanderpool asked, his voice a pained whisper, his eyes so swollen he looked like a day old pup.

"Morning," Taulbee replied, feeling the rasp in his own throat. "Roll out and help me clean this mess."

Roe uncoiled slowly from the floor and began to fold the covers he'd stripped from Taulbee's bed. He was tall and thin, his only fat in the form of a beer belly that filled the waist of his baggy jeans like a pregnancy. He had bad teeth, a stringy beard, and long stringy hair that he kept bundled under a cap.

By noon they had cleared all the emptied beer cans and wine and whiskey bottles from the front room, dumped the ashtrays, and picked through the carpet for broken glass.

Taulbee had just plugged in the vacuum when he looked out the window to see his Aunt Madge leading a delegation from her church up his front porch steps. He called out a warning to Roe who stepped into the hall closet and shut the door.

Taulbee bit off a curse, sighed, and opened the door at the first forceful knock. His Aunt Madge marched in without hesitation. She was a heavyset woman in a sweat dampened print dress that hung nearly to her ankles. A sheen of sweat covered her face and arms.

The others, including Brother Bill Singleton, lingered on the threshold until Taulbee bid them enter. "Come in, come in," he said, willing himself to grip each man and woman by the hand and speak their names in greeting. "Mrs. Cousins. Mr. Green. Brother Singelton. Eula Mae. Forgive the mess. I'm in the midst of my Sunday house cleaning."

"There's more than houses need cleansed on this Sunday," Eula Mae said. Taulbee chose not to reply. Instead, he said, "You all make yourselves at home. Can you stay while I put on coffee?"

Ed Green's face relaxed at the mention of coffee, and when Taulbee offered up his grandmother's apple spice cake even Brother Singleton seemed to waver in his resolve.

But Madge cut him off. "Never mind," she said. "None of that." The entire delegation situated themselves, three abreast on the couch and one in each armchair, so that Taulbee alone was left standing.

Taulbee looked around as if to find another chair, then

pulled the ottoman from its place before Ed Green and, with his long legs splayed before him, settled on that. His apparent ease angered Madge so much she could not restrain a swipe at his legs with her funeral home fan.

The delegation remained quiet while sneaking glances at Brother Singleton who sat stiffly forward with his hands clasped. When the tension got to be too much, Taulbee slapped Ed Green's knee and asked, "How's your garden growing?"

Ed Green looked at Brother Singleton, then he smiled nervously. "My peas have done better this year than they ever have," he said. "My tomatoes look blighted though. I can't figure out why."

"Weather's been good," Taulbee said.

Madge's impatient groan silenced them. She cleared her throat and said, "Brother Singleton."

"Taulbee," Brother Singleton began, "the good book says whoever is deceived by strong drink is not wise."

"The body is the Lord's temple," Eula Mae added.

"Take heed lest your heart be overcharged with drunkenness," said Brother Singleton, "for as a snare it shall come on all those that dwell on the face of the earth."

"Yeah," Taulbee said. "I believe those words." Then he turned to Ed Green again. "You plant any corn and beans this year?"

"Taulbee," Aunt Madge said. "We're not here to speak of gardening."

Taulbee drew in his legs and crossed them at the ankles. He crossed his arms and said, "Do you reckon there's more than one kind of drunkenness? I mean, is there more than one kind of snare? Help me out on this, Eula Mae. Do you reckon them cigarettes you all smoke before and after preaching might be as much a snare as strong drink?"

"The Bible don't say nothing about cigarettes," Eula Mae replied. She was a middle-aged woman, all skin and bone, with tightly bundled gray hair and nicotine stained fingers.

"But ain't it the same?" Taulbee asked.

"We're all sinners in the sight of the Lord," Brother Singleton said. "The Lord forgives all sinners, but you have to ask for it."

Madge cleared things up. "Them that goes to church are saved," she said. "Them that lays out drunk every night are damned."

"I don't believe a man has to go to church to get religion," Taulbee argued. "You don't know but what I don't read my Bible regular."

Madge smirked, looking past Taulbee. "They's evidence against you knowing the proper use of scripture," she said. She nudged Brother Singleton, who frowned at something past Taulbee's seeing. Taulbee looked over his shoulder, saw nothing at first but the open window, the porch and empty yard beyond. On second glance he saw that the book he'd propped the window with was the hard bound bible his aunt had given him at his father's funeral. He began to wish that he had smoked either more or less dope.

"Don't take this wrong, Taulbee," Brother Singleton continued. "We're not here to condemn you. We're your friends and neighbors, and we're just concerned is all, about where your life is headed."

"Ruination is where it's headed," Aunt Madge muttered.

"You used to be a good churchgoer," Eula Mae said.

"We know how it's been since Thurman passed on," Ed Green said.

"How's it been, Ed?" Taulbee asked. He waved the question off when he saw the look on Ed Green's face. "I appreciate your-all's concern," he said. "I remember you-all praying for Dad. I appreciate that. And I'm not making out like I've not backslid here lately, but they's some things a body has to come around to on their own terms. The Lord knows what's in me whether you-all can see it or not."

Aunt Madge sighed and shook her head. She stood suddenly, took a step toward the door, then paused. The rest of the delegation hurriedly rose to follow. "You know where we meet," Brother Singleton said, reaching for Taulbee's hand. "You know you're welcome any time."

Madge stood by the doorway until the others had gone out, then she leaned close to Taulbee and whispered, "How you think Thurman would feel if he could see you now?"

Roe Vanderpool stepped from his hiding place when they were all gone. "What was that about?" he asked.

"Busybodies," was all Taulbee replied.

Taulbee started the workweek the next morning with his usual ritual, slipping his hand inside the wheel well of the truck he and Roe used to haul garbage, rocking the cab up and down on his shoulder while he felt for the latch that would release it. Then he swung the cab forward over the engine and propped it in place. He added a quart of oil without bothering to check the level. He pulled each plug wire, wiped it and the plug, then reconnected them firmly.

He squeezed the radiator hoses, looking for fresh cracks, taping any he found. He checked around the clamps. As he added hydraulic fluid he made the usual vow to himself that next weekend he and Roe would fly in and fix whatever seal kept leaking. Then he eased the cab back over the engine and latched it down. He climbed up into the cab, pumped the hydraulic clutch, and turned the ignition.

After a few grinds of the flywheel, the truck started. It was a 1965 GMC that he and Roe had bought at auction. They had overhauled the engine as best they could, then scrapped the rusted out bed and hammered together a new one from cast-off railroad ties and two-by-fours and three-quarter inch plywood. Between tinkering and taping and cursing, it ran well enough to complete the weekly garbage run they had contracted from the county.

Half a mile down the road Taulbee stopped before a weatherworn trailer and blew what passed for the truck's horn, its sound like the low-toned moo of a sickly cow. Roe came from the trailer carrying a lunch box in one hand and a small radio in the other. He climbed slow motion into the cab and hung the radio from the rear view mirror. He tuned to a country station, fiddling with the volume until Billy Ray Cyrus' toneless twang rose above the rattle of the truck's engine. He said "good morning" and the two were off on their day's run.

The first few stops were slow going, Roe barely rousing himself from the truck to help toss on the bags of garbage. By the time they reached the mouth of Smith's Fork, the halfway point of their run, they were both fully awake, sweating as much from the heat of the engine that rose from beneath the cab as from their morning's work. Roe produced their customary joint as they left the main highway and said his first words since "good morning."

"I'd give my left nut for a cold beer."

"Is that all you think about?" Taulbee asked. "It's not even 12 o'clock."

"These Mondays wear hard."

"I believe Aunt Madge should pay you a visit."

"I think not."

The cab filled with the weedy smoke of homegrown pot. Taulbee, feeling the creeping tendrils of a headache in his temples, considered for a moment the exchange of Roe's left nut for a cold anything. While he thirsted he thought of his Aunt Madge's question: "What would his father think of him?"

"Work hard," his father had told him when he was a boy, just after his mother had died, "so you'll have something of your own." His father had worked nearly thirty years in the coal mines, then had a stroke the year before he'd planned to retire. He'd suffered a few days in the hospital, at one point whispering in a moment of drugged consciousness for Taulbee to find Jesus.

Taulbee's baptism had been his father's dying wish. That he'd turned from the church in the months since seemed no more a betrayal than his vow never to enter the mines again. Coal mining and Jesus had been his father's life.

"I could use a cold pop," Taulbee said.

They had finished the joint by the time they reached their next pickup, Roe having swallowed the roach as a precaution against its evidence. They were stoned enough not to mind the stink of rancid meat, of rotted greens, and whatever varied spoilage rose with the swarm of midday flies around the heavy bags of garbage. When one bag burst open to spill soggy coffee grounds, egg shells, cabbage leaves, onion peels, carrot tops, crusted soup cans, and other bits of unidentifiable food remnants and household refuse onto their shoes, they said in unison, "I love this job." Then they scooped up the spill with shovels, scraped off their shoes, and went their way.

At the next pickup, Polly Huff stood waiting next to her trash. She was a short, plump old woman. An Old Regular Baptist, she wore her nearly waist length gray hair in a loose bun that bobbed a little as she waved to Taulbee and Roe from the roadside. "I need you boys to help me," she said, when Taulbee pulled the truck onto the shoulder of the road and cut the engine. "The old man's down in his legs today."

Taulbee and Roe hopped from the cab and followed the old woman up her unpaved driveway to the little single story white house that sat hidden behind a pair of weeping willow trees and a rock wall covered with honeysuckle vines. Taulbee breathed deeply when he passed the honeysuckle. He considered plucking a flower to suck the nectar from its cup.

Polly's husband sat in his age worn recliner, his feet cushioned by a pillow. He was dressed in dark blue trousers and a white short sleeved shirt buttoned nearly to the collar.

"How you doing, Marvin?" Taulbee asked.

"I'm wanting to sit on the porch," Marvin replied, "and these old legs are too give out to get me there."

"We'll get you there," Taulbee said. He and Roe stood on either side of Marvin's chair while Marvin draped an arm around each one's shoulders, then they slipped their hands gently under his legs and lifted.

Polly held the door while they carried him to the porch, fretting that they might bump his legs against the door frame or the banister rails or that they might drop him altogether. "Be careful, now," she said. "Careful."

They settled him easily into his rocking chair, and Polly raised his feet to a stool. "Thank you, boys, thank you," Marvin said. "Now I can sit and watch the day go by."

"Anything else we can help with?" Taulbee asked.

Marvin waved them off. "How's the garbage business?"

"Ain't no shortage of garbage," Roe answered.

"Be a bad sign if there was," Marvin said. He threaded his fingers together and cupped his hands behind his head, leaning back in the rocker. "You and your daddy was both miners?"

"Yes," Taulbee replied.

"I believe I worked with him over at Yellow Creek, or it might have been Consolidated," Marvin said. "He ever mention that?"

"He might have."

"They's times I miss being underground," Marvin said. "I miss the fellers I worked with."

"We have to go," Taulbee said.

"Take them tomatoes." Marvin pointed to a paper sack full of ripe tomatoes on the steps. He raised his hand. "Remind me to your daddy."

Polly called out a "God bless" as Roe and Taulbee walked down the steps.

When they were in the truck, Roe said, "I hope I ain't never in that shape."

"Marvin does all right," Taulbee said.

"He ain't got no mind no more," Roe said.

"He remembers Dad."

"He wouldn't know your dad from Adam. Thinks he's still yet living."

The truck lurched as Taulbee pumped the clutch. He ground the shift into second, and they rolled down the road to the next pickup.

An hour later they pulled off at the base of Polk Mountain and had their lunch. They sat in the hot cab with the doors open and ate bologna on white bread with cans of half-cold soda. They ate the entire sack of tomatoes, the juice dripping down their chins and fingers as they bit open the ripe skins and swallowed the tangy pulp. Afterwards they washed with the ice melt from their cooler.

Roe produced another joint. They smoked it furtively, keeping the radio turned low so they could listen for any approaching cars.

"I'd not miss this job," Roe said as they pulled back onto the road.

"You'd miss getting paid," Taulbee said.

"I'd go on the draw."

"I don't believe in welfare."

"You don't believe in nothing."

Taulbee drove back the way they had come for a quarter of a mile, to the top of small hill, then he turned the truck at the mouth of a logging road and headed it back down the grade, building speed for the climb up Polk Mountain. They hit the upgrade in fourth gear. Taulbee kept the gas floored and when the truck began to slow he downshifted to third. The truck regained its speed for a while, but as the grade increased it slowed again. Near the mountain's crest Taulbee shifted to second. The truck shuddered and groaned, barely pulling itself upward. Then, about the time Roe asked if he should jump out and push, it topped the mountain.

"They's worse things than welfare," Roe said. "This job among them."

"I'll work for my living," Taulbee said as the truck picked up speed down the mountain.

After work and a shower, Taulbee drove his father's pickup to the holler where his grandmother lived. She was eighty years old and a widow, though she still lived on her own in the house where she had raised five children. Of the three that still lived, Madge was the only one near home.

Taulbee spent an hour hoeing the weeds from the patch of corn he'd planted. Then he dug a few potatoes, pulled some onions, and picked a sack full of peas for their supper.

"Aunt Madge came to see me," Taulbee said as they sat on the porch after they'd eaten in the first cool moments of dusk. "She's got ideas about running my life."

"Madge loves you," his grandmother replied. "That's how she knows to show it." The runners of her chair squeaked as she rocked back and forth. She was a slight woman with snow white hair and lively eyes, the skin of her face and forearms as brown as a nut. Her forearms were long and slender, her hands, though heavily veined, were still young looking. She held a cane idly across her lap.

"It don't matter what I do or don't do," Taulbee said. "It's all wrong to her. I don't live my life to suit other people."

"You don't live it to spite them either," his grandmother replied.

"Madge thinks church is the answer to it all."

"I'll not fault Madge for being a churchgoer."

"Bunch of hypocrites."

Taulbee had forgotten the remnant of strength in his grandmother's hands. He didn't see the cane flicking out, surprisingly fast and accurate, to rap him between his shoulders. "That's spiteful talk," his grandmother said. She continued rocking until Taulbee settled warily into his chair again.

"It may be she sees more of your daddy in you than she ought to, and she ought not judge you like she does, but she's not false to what she believes."

"Why don't you go to church?" Taulbee asked.

"I live my deal with the Lord," his grandmother said. "Don't you doubt it."

At the end of the next workday as they unloaded their haul at the county dump, Roe told Taulbee they could get some pot if they stopped off at the house of a fellow Roe knew.

"I'm awfully tired," Taulbee said.

"What?" Roe said. "You know you always like some good smoke."

"I been thinking about cutting back," Taulbee said.

"Cut back tomorrow," Roe said. "I told Johnny we'd be there."

Johnny lived five miles up a holler on a road that branched off to become little more than an unpaved, deeply rutted trail. Where the road ran into a shallow creek, they stopped the truck and got out to walk.

"Don't get us lost," Taulbee said.

They waded the creek, then climbed a path by a kudzu

matted fence. Roe stopped when they spotted the house. When he called out his buddy's name, several dogs began barking from an enclosed kennel at the side of the house. Moments later a man came onto the porch. He was short with shaggy blonde hair and beard, his blue work shirt barely stretching across his belly which rode atop the waistband of his jeans. He stared for a moment then waved them on.

Later over pipe bowls of homegrown sinsemilla Roe negotiated his purchase, his friend weighing out the Baggie on a postal scale. "I've got over a hundred plants," Johnny said, "spread in twos and threes all over the hills, no one big patch to see from the air. That all comes in, I'll have an easy winter."

"I wouldn't mind bringing in a big crop," Roe said. "A few pounds of pot would set a man up for years."

"It's the thieves you have to watch for," Johnny said, "and the deer. You can pay off the law."

Taulbee sat quietly, listening to their schemes for easy riches. The year his father died, he'd quit the mines and gone to Indiana to work on an assembly line in an appliance factory. He'd made good money then, but seen nothing in Indiana worth building his life around. He'd wasted the money and returned home as broke and aimless as when he'd left.

Ever since he'd gone from scheme to scheme, working indifferently at whatever he happened into. He and Roe had teamed up on every half-assed work crew in the county. They had laid block, cut weeds along roadways and gas company pipelines. They had carpentered and drywalled. In another year, when their garbage hauling venture collapsed, he could see them tending their own marijuana crop, sweating out the season in fear of helicopters, setting traps for the thieves, both human and animal, that would pilfer their livelihood.

Taulbee pinched another bowl full from the bud Johnny had supplied for their sampling. It had become easier for him to get high, so thick was his blood with pot. Sometimes even the thought of marijuana, its recollected smell, would stone him as thoroughly as a bong hit. Being stoned made his life seemed better lived, the uncertainty of his future less significant.

In a little while the heaviness of Taulbee's mind lifted, and he thought of nothing more than the pleasure of good cultivation. He began to laugh. Roe and Johnny stopped their talk and laughed with him.

What he remembered about the rest of the night were clouds of smoke and laughter. He remembered backing the truck nearly a quarter mile to find a place in the road wide enough to turn, and he remembered Roe stumbling into a ditch as he tried to act as guide.

The next afternoon, when the first of his customers called to complain that their garbage had not been collected, Taulbee claimed equipment failure, then he unplugged the phone and went back to sleep.

For the rest of the week Taulbee and Roe worked longer shifts to make up for their one lost day. By late Friday evening they had managed to collect all the garbage for which they had contracted. They bought a case of beer to celebrate the workweek's end and went to Taulbee's house to drink it.

By midnight the regular party crew had arrived. Had he stayed with beer and pot, with possibly a Xanax for the hangover, Taulbee would've survived the night without illness. But when Sammy produced a quart of moonshine, Taulbee knew there was no out for him but sickness and suffering. So rare and so costly had the genuine stuff become that Taulbee could not refuse a drink, and after his first he could not refuse another.

For a short time the potent, nearly pure alcohol heightened Taulbee's buzz. He talked wildly, swinging his arms, clapping his hands together like a preacher in the throes of spiritual zeal.

"Take heed," he shouted, "lest you be overcome." He tried to climb upon a chair, was prevented by several hands. "Take heed," he shouted. "Strong drink is a snare." He raised a smoldering joint. "Take heed lest you be overcome with drunkenness and the cares of this life."

The regular crew laughed as Taulbee spun around the room in the mania of his sermon. He stumbled across chairs, fell headlong into huddles of his fellow drinkers, was passed from hand to hand until he could be settled in an out of the way corner. "Strong drink is a snare," he shouted. "Be not deceived."

In the moments before unconsciousness a thought occurred to him, and he called Roe to his side. "Is this this weekend or last?" he asked. He passed out before Roe could answer.

Taulbee's recovery lasted the remainder of the weekend, in which time he swore off all drink and smoke and even food, everything but water, which he drank by the pitcher.

When his aunt Madge came to visit on Sunday afternoon

he was too weak to contend against her. He meekly endured her prayers and scathing grief at the loss of his soul. But when she told him how he'd disgraced his father's memory, he rose from the couch and said, "I don't have to listen to this."

"Your daddy was a good, hard working man," she said. "A sober, hard working Christian man. And you've come to nothing but drink and idleness."

"I work," Taulbee said. When he tried to push past his aunt to the door, he stumbled, and Madge was knocked against the door frame. It had been a light, accidental contact, yet Madge reacted as if he'd struck with purpose and force. She burst into shocked tears, struck at him with her hand, and left the house.

By that night he'd heard from nearly every family member he had. His Uncle Trace phoned from Dayton, Ohio. He offered advice on temperance and suggested a move to where there was a better chance for work, like Dayton, Ohio. His great-aunt Bertha phoned from her nursing home sickbed. She called him a little shitass in a quavering voice. His twelve year old first cousin came to his door and threatened to beat him up. The only person who didn't call was his grandmother, and Taulbee took that as a worse sign than if she had. By the time they had all had their say Taulbee was so sick at heart he agreed to attend a church meeting in hopes of making amends.

His outlook was not improved the next morning when he tried to start the garbage truck and heard the pained clatter of a cracked engine block. He and Roe spent the day tinkering with the now useless scrap of an engine. Taulbee contented himself with cigarettes while Roe smoked the last of his pot. By evening they had run through all the new schemes they could think of, deciding at last to sell the truck for scrap and look for other means of support.

Madge was the first to greet Taulbee at the Left Fork Baptist Church. She smiled and hugged him as she had not in years. Taulbee was surprised at her lack of anger. Eula Mae greeted him next, the beginning of real tears at the corners of her eyes. Ed Green slapped him on the back. Brother Singleton shook his hand firmly and welcomed him back to the fold. It was as if his simple presence in church atoned for his sinfulness. In their eyes he had made a choice.

Ed Green put a hand on Taulbee's arm as they took their seats. "I've got my permit to mine that Beaver Creek property," he said. "I'll put you on."

"I don't know," Taulbee said.

"You think it over," Ed said. "Your old daddy was a good church member."

They sang 'Throw Out the Lifeline' to begin the meeting, then Brother Singleton stood before the podium. He looked sternly into his open Bible for what seemed a long time, then he began to preach. "God is the light," he shouted. "And in him is no darkness."

"Amen," someone called. Cardboard fans, painted with scenes of the resurrection or the last supper, fluttered like bird wings among the congregation.

"Who walks in darkness walks in sin."

Brother Singleton had preached the funeral for Taulbee's father. He had prayed over his bed in the hospital.

"If we say we have no sin, the truth is not in us. We are

forgiven and cleansed of all unrighteousness if we confess our sins."

Taulbee thought of the accidents he'd seen around mines, men taking a misstep (their minds on supper, a woman, weekend fishing) and getting killed or maimed by some piece of machinery they'd worked safely around for years. He thought how his father had worked thirty years without a scratch, kept his mind on work and Jesus.

He remembered the one bad roof fall he'd seen, had just missed being in. He'd been on the shift before, had come out on the same mantrip the dead men went in on. He was still at the mine when the accident happened. He remembered the long hours of the rescue operation, the relief at seeing the few survivors brought up on stretchers, injured but alive, the grief when all those others were brought up in body bags.

Taulbee had worked a long time with those miners. He could see them in the congregation around him, the features of the dead carried on in the faces of the living. He thought about how Madge saw his father in him.

"The blood of Jesus Christ, his son, cleanseth us from sin."

If he left to find work, it would be in a place that would never be home no matter how long he lived there. If he kept on as he had with Roe, picking up work as he could, he would smoke dope and drink until he was too old for any other kind of life. If he went back in the mines.... He thought about the bodies of those dead miners. He looked at the people around him. A few were blank faced, their heads nodding, eyelids flickering in their struggle to keep wakeful, but most were caught up in the vigor of Brother

Singleton's sermon, their eyes bright, their heads bent forward to hear, their faith evident. Taulbee knew that what he wanted was in the faces of these people. He wanted to believe as they believed in something worth the pain of living.

Half an hour into the sermon Taulbee felt a sudden pang of thirst. "Strong drink is as a snare," he thought.

The sermon lasted another three-quarters of an hour. When it ended the congregation sang 'The Old Rugged Cross.'

Taulbee stayed for the church supper. He ate fried chicken and drank lemonade, his appetite approved by everyone around him. When he walked out the church door that evening, he felt the good graces of the entire congregation go with him, like so many ghostly voices guiding his will. Even so he thirsted for a beer all that night.

EULOGY

Tara slowed as she passed the small gas station. Her gas gauge showed just above empty, but when she saw the group of shaggy haired men in overalls and tattered jeans, she sped on.

On a road that curved like a snake, she passed brick ranch houses and prefab log homes, tarpaper shacks and weather stained trailers. Where the road rose to the ridge lines, she looked down on the tinny sparkle of the trailer where her family had lived before her father got his money. It sat half-buried beneath a bank of mud from the strip mine.

Her car squealed into the curves, blaring rap to the spring trees. Near the top of one high ridge, it slowed, dropping down a gear and coming to a near stop. Then it topped the highest hill and fell in a swift glide into the next valley.

The Right Fork Revival Church sat on a grassy flat between the bend of the road and the creek for which it was named. So many were at the gathering that their cars choked the narrow highway to a single lane of traffic. Tara squeezed her Miata between the high bumpers of a sixties Oldsmobile and a sleek new Buick, locking the door by habit as she got out.

Much of the congregation had spilled into the yard and gathered in groups to talk. Her mother, Ester, pale and plump in black silk, met her at the church door. "Tara," she said, "Baby, I've worried and I've worried. I'm so glad you got here safe."

"Mommy," Tara said, lightly touching her mother's cheek with her own.

A tired looking man in a pinstripe suit moved forward to grasp Tara's hand. He guided them into the church.

Ester held Tara's arm as they walked. "I have your room all ready," she whispered.

"I have to be back for school tomorrow," Tara replied.

Her grandmother's coffin was set before the small stage at the back of the church. The stage held the podium and a half circle of canvas backed folding chairs. Of the men seated there, idly studying their hymnals, Tara could name Luther Sloane, Denver Stidham, and Jack Collins. As she settled into the pews between her mother and father, Wade Tolliver walked by, pausing to greet each family member before ascending the stage.

"Brothers and sisters," he said as he came before the podium, his square bricklayer's hands raised in the air, "it is indeed a blessing to see so many gathered here today to share fellowship in this time of sorrow. So many family members and dear friends come together as once again death has visited one of our homes. We will miss our dear sister, Ruth. We will miss her voice joined together in prayer with ours, and we will miss her generous spirit and the grace of her Christian devotion. We may take comfort in knowing that this woman who saw her own beloved husband and two of five beloved children pass before her, who saw grief and hardship in life and yet always walked with the Lord, abides now with the Lord."

"But I wonder, brothers and sisters, how many of us,

gathered here today, if old death should call, would be as ready in spirit as our dear sister Ruth. As is so often the case, so many of the friends we see here today, we see only in the times of sorrow and not of gladness. Brothers and sisters, how many of those gathered here today, those who are loved on this earth, father and son, mother and daughter, near and dear in heart but lost in spirit, will be found wanting when Judgment comes? How many, brothers and sisters, feel not the light of Jesus in their hearts? It is a narrow way, brothers and sisters, to the gates of paradise and a hard road that only a chosen few may travel. How many here have strayed, brothers and sisters, as lambs lost to the flock, have taken paths away from family, from God, and from life eternal? Let us bow our heads and pray now, brothers and sisters, not for the soul of dear Ruth, for she is safe in the bosom of her Lord, but for the soul of each man, woman, and child gathered here today."

Tara stared grimly at her lap as the congregation held a moment of silent prayer. When the brothers started on 'The Old Rugged Cross,' she slipped on her sunglasses. She bowed her head and tried to close her ears to 'Rock of Ages' and 'The Great Speckled Bird.' When the singing was over, she went with her parents to stand by the coffin. Her father's thin neck barely filled his shirt collar. He looked pale and lost.

One by one, the relatives approached, pausing to speak their few words. Some embraced Tara. Others just squeezed her hand.

"Is this Tara? I never would have recognized her."

"What a pretty girl."

Tara smiled, trading stiff hugs with half-remembered aunts

and distant cousins. "Are you still yet in school?" asked an uncle by marriage. "What are you going to make?"

"I'm studying Sociology," Tara explained.

It was only after the mob of kinship had passed that she made herself look into the coffin to see the pale remains of her grandmother who looked better in death than in the last year of her life.

They rode in silence to the family cemetery. Wade Tolliver stood at the head of the grave as they lowered in the coffin. He read from a large, white Bible, its pages fluttering in a light breeze that flipped Tara's hair into her eyes and caused her to hold her dress tightly against her knees.

"Blessed be God," he read. "Who comforteth us in all our tribulations, that we may be able to comfort them which are in any trouble, by the comfort wherewith we ourselves are comforted by God. For as the sufferings of Christ abound in us, so our consolation also aboundeth by Christ." Then he closed the Bible, and as he spoke the last words some of the crowd spoke with him.

"I am the resurrection and the life," they said. "He that believeth in me, though he were dead, yet shall he live. And whosoever liveth and believeth in me shall never die. Amen."

The family members slowly edged away, some with sorrowful good-byes, others with nods and waves. Soon Tara and her parents were left to themselves by the open grave, alone but for the workmen who leaned patiently on their shovels next to the mound of loose dirt.

A dulcimer hung over the living room fireplace of the new house. Cornshuck dolls crowded the mantel. A birch bark rocker sat next to a barrel-shaped table that held a collection of cedar bowls. On one wall hung a patchwork quilt, on another, a poster size picture of her grandfather next to a thick-horned bull in a pasture full of rocks.

Tara sat on the edge of the couch next to her mother. Her father, Tom, slumped in the rocker, his tie pulled loose, his suit jacket clutched in his lap. His lips trembled before he spoke. "Tara," he said, "do you need anything?"

"No."

Tom looked quickly at the floor. His lips trembled slightly, but he said nothing.

"The service was very nice," Tara said as Ester squeezed her hand.

"Ruth would've liked the sermon," Ester said. "She's in peace now. It was a relief for her to pass. I mean for her it was a relief. We tried to provide the best for her we could. I guess we give her all we could."

Tom rose from the rocker. "I've got to change clothes," he mumbled and walked slowly from the room.

"He ain't sleeping at all," Ester whispered.

It was still light when Tara went to her father's work shed. He sat at his bench, filing the rust from an antique breast auger. The shed's walls were covered with the old-time tools that he found at flea markets. He'd changed into a pair of khaki pants and a wrong looking sweater that she knew had been her mother's choosing. He looked older, by years and years, as old as her grandfather in his picture.

"Daddy," she said.

Tom smiled broadly as he turned. His hands and the cuffs of the ugly sweater were stained with rust.

"Are you okay?" she asked.

"I will be," he said, "by and by."

"Mommy made supper."

Tom looked down at his hands, began to pluck at his sweater cuffs. "Do you have to leave?" he asked.

"Yes," she said.

"Will you tell me if you need anything?"

"Yes."

"It's so nice to sit down like a family," Ester said. She smiled and ate her dinner in small bites. Her hand trembled a little, and from time to time she dabbed her napkin to her eyes.

Tara watched her father force bites of food. "I passed the homeplace," she said. "There's not much left after they strip-mined."

Her father laid his knife and fork across his plate and pushed it away. "It liked to killed Mommy to lease that coal," he said.

"They're going to reclaim it, though," Ester said. "Sow it over in grass and make pastureland. Your daddy's going to have cattle on it."

Tara folded her napkin and laid it carefully on the table. For a moment she remembered the old times, the small trailer that broiled in the summer and froze in the winter, that rocked in the wind all year round. She remembered her and her mother gardening, cooking the beans and corn and cabbage to can for the winter. She remembered her father coming in from his job covered in dirt and grease, too tired almost to eat or wash, and her mother putting on a red smock and going to her job at a grocery, her mother going out as her father came in.

Her parents fell silent as Tara rose from her chair. Her father stared at the table, his face rigid. A tremor crossed her mother's face. She took a heavy breath and raised her napkin to her eyes.

"I have to go," Tara said.

"Do you need anything?" Tom asked.

"No."

Before she left, her father loaded a sack of new potatoes, two bags of green onions, and early peas in the back seat of her car, then pressed money into her hand.

Tara's fuel light came on just before she reached the main road. She had thought to make it up the last big hill then coast down to the station she had passed earlier, but she got only halfway before the car stalled and she rolled back to the bottom.

She steered off the road onto a shoulder in front of a run-down trailer. She sat in the car and tried the ignition for a few minutes, but there was too little fuel to even turn the motor. She got out slowly, watching the shadows move behind the trailer's curtains.

The porch light flicked on as she entered the yard, and a young man came out, big and rough looking in a ragged flannel shirt and greasy jeans worn thin as paper. When he saw her, he stopped and stared, shoulders stooped, hands in pockets.

Tara took a step back. When he didn't move, she found her voice. "Could you help me?" She pointed to her car. "I'm out of gas."

The man shrugged and stepped down into the yard, coming so close that Tara could smell him. When he was close enough to touch her, another form, slight and stiff and a little crooked, came from the trailer. "Who's that now?" said a gruff voice. "Davey?"

"I'm out of gas," Tara said again.

The old man had thick gray hair cut in a burr around his sallow, thin-skinned face. He wore baggy work pants and a sleeveless undershirt, his thin arms covered with tattoos, an anchor on each forearm, a wrinkled heart on the shrunken biceps of his right arm, and what was either an X or a misshapen cross on the back of either hand.

"What's that?" he asked when he stood before Tara.

"I'm out of gas," she said.

The old man studied her for a moment. Then he turned. "Davey," he said "take my car and get this girl some gas!"

Davey walked slowly around the side of the trailer, near the hitch, and wrenched open the door of a rust colored hatchback. The door screamed on its hinges, the car sinking a little as Davey slid his weight behind the steering wheel.

"I can pay you," Tara said.

The old man held up his hand. He turned his head to one side and slowly turned his body toward the trailer. "Sis," he called. "Sissy. Come take a ride." A girl with long blonde hair and a familiar seeming face darted out of the trailer. She paused just a moment to look at Tara then climbed into the back seat of the car. It had backed onto the highway in a cloud of gassy fumes. The passenger side door stood open.

Tara stared at the stained and threadbare seat for a few seconds before she got in.

The little car climbed the hill slowly, its muffler roaring so hard that Tara could feel it through the floor. She pulled her skirt about her knees and shifted her weight, but the seat was too battered for comfort.

The interior light was stuck on, casting a pale sheen throughout the car. She watched Davey drive, his face and body lax, his hands barely seeming to grip the steering wheel, his eyes shifting from the road to the dark tree lines to the hazy twilight hillsides.

"Thanks for helping," she said and realized that the pained roar of the car had drowned her words. She tried to roll down her window. When it wouldn't budge, she stared straight ahead, breathing slowly through her mouth.

When they reached the station, Davey took a plastic milk jug from the back seat. "You'll have to buy the gas," he said.

Tara blushed when the attendant inside the station asked, "Are you with them?" She paid for the gas, bought a candy bar, and walked silently back to the car. She offered the candy to the girl.

The girl glanced at Davey and shook her head no. The ride back seemed quicker. Tara felt safer after having bought the jug of gasoline, though she still watched Davey from the corner of her eye.

When they got back to the trailer, Davey handed her the jug and a rubber hose. She hesitated, then opened the gas cap on her car. She slipped the hose inside and tried to pour the gas into the end.

"No," Davey said. He moved toward her, his hands outstretched. She gasped, stepping quickly away. Davey hesitated. He dropped his hands, clenched them at his sides, then he reached them toward her, palms up. Tara handed him the jug and hose. He slipped the hose into the jug and sucked on the end until the gas began to siphon out, then he slipped the hose into the tank, and the gas slowly emptied from the jug.

"I wish you'd let me pay you," Tara said when she was in her car. The girl stood by her door. The old man stood next to the girl, his hand on her shoulder. Davey sat on the steps beside an old woman in knit slacks and a sleeveless white top. The old man held up his hand. "No," he said, "that's all right. I might need you to help me sometime."

Tara smiled and waved as she drove off. She didn't stop to fill her tank until she reached Hazard. By the time she reached Jackson, she had begun to cry a little. She sped through Breathitt County with her windows open, the cold night air whipping through the car. Just before Campton, she pulled off the road, lowered her head and cried full out.

THE IDEA OF IT

I tell my boy stories about growing up here. I ask him whether he wouldn't like a pony, like I had when I was his age. He says he'd rather have a motorcycle, one he could ride down to Florida. We're on the hillside above the cow pasture. The tin roof of the barn flashes sunlight at us whenever the cloud cover breaks.

"Florida is hot in August," I say.

"So is Kentucky," he replies.

We've cleared the brush around the house and barn lot, but the pasture is still thick with horse weeds, poison ivy, kudzu and sprouts of beech, sassafras, maple, and pine. I've considered buying goats for the sake of the kudzu and ivy.

"Making it okay?" I ask my boy.

Gabriel shrugs, pulls up some clumps of grass to toss at a ground squirrel that has popped up from the roots of a near-by oak tree. He's not used to this outside work. His face is red, and I'm afraid he's sick from being in the sun too much.

"How'd you like a cold drink of water?" I ask.

"We didn't bring any," he says.

"I mean some good spring water. Best water you ever drunk." I stand and motion for him to follow me up the hill. He sighs, as if I'm calling him to some hard task, and rises.

The spring I'm remembering ran from the last frost of

winter to the first dry spell of summer, as cold as it was clean tasting. In springtime it roared, spewing white foam over rocks and logs. In summer it ran so quiet there was barely a sound to tell its whereabouts.

We used to come upon it in our play, call time-out from our pretend hunts and headlong chases to drink cowboy style from the wild water. We made dams from sticks and mud, boats from twigs and leaves, saw gemstones in water-smoothed pebbles, one game passing to the next in days that went with no in-between from the first of summer to the last.

It's likely dry now, but I'm betting the little bit of rain we've had this week will have left enough of a trickle to wet our throats. The only water Gabriel has ever drunk has been flavored by metal pipes and fluoride.

It's a hard climb over the ridge to the holler where I remember the spring running. Gabriel doesn't talk. He breathes hard, and I stop a few times to give him rest before he asks for it. I want to carry him because of how hard he's working, but then again I don't because of how old he's grown and because I want him to get the benefit of the climb.

"You'll get used to it," I tell him. "You'll be climbing these hills like a mountain goat."

"I guess," he says.

The steep hill burns my thigh muscles. Near the top I have to angle sideways and dig the edges of my boots against the slope to keep upright. Gabriel slips a few times, and I have to reach my hand to help him, each time pulling him a little past where he'd lost his ground.

"Ain't nothing worthwhile comes easy," I say.

He doesn't answer, and in another minute we top the hill. We rest on one of the boulders that lie like the bones of a spine along the ridge tops. We look where the holler should be. What we see is bare ground, blasted rock, splintered trees, slate and low grade coal like black gore spilled from a wound. What we see is a pond filled with black water, runoff from a strip mine.

I've been told about the ten acres Grandpa leased for stripping. I've seen it before now, but I've not connected its location with the memory of my spring.

Gabriel wrinkles his nose at the rank water. "Are we going to drink that?" he asks.

"No," I say. "We're not going to drink that."

The best part of my childhood was spent on this farm here in eastern Kentucky. My dad worked in the mines then. Mom, Dad and me all lived here with Grandma and Grandpa. When I was ten Dad moved Mom and me to Dayton, Ohio. He got a job in a Frigidaire factory. He didn't stick with it though, or it didn't stick with him. After about a year we moved again, to Indianapolis, then the next year to Detroit, then to Pittsburgh, then to Cincinnati.

I'm not making out like those were bad years. We were not unhappy as a family, just unsettled like. I guess that being unsettled is what's kept with me most. Even after I married Cathy and we had our first kid, I couldn't be still. We've lived all over the midwest and even in California for a while, me taking whatever work I happened into, Cathy and little Gabriel dragging along behind. For a long while now, I've been scared of reliving my father's life.

127

The main thing I want is for my kids, Gabriel and the little one we have on the way, to know what it is to grow up in one place, to know one place as home.

Wherever we've lived, I've thought of the steep pasture behind the barn and Grandma's old milk cow standing under a shade tree still as a picture.

When Grandma died last year and left the farm to Dad, I scraped up all my savings and offered to buy him out. He said "no." It wasn't that he was going to come back and live here himself. Mom would've never left Cincinnati. But he didn't want to give up the idea of it.

"I know what you mean," I said. "How about I go live there and pay rent?"

He agreed to that. In a week we had packed all we cared for and made our move.

I've put in applications from here to Wayland. Whenever I go to look it's like I'm some kind of foreigner come in to take away somebody else's livelihood, somebody with more right to a living than me. When I speak these local boys roll their eyes at each other. They grunt and ask me where I'm from. I have to tell myself not to get mad. There's men who've lived here all their lives can't get any nearer a paycheck than me. There's talk of wage cuts and layoffs at the mines. Nobody's hiring.

I haven't worked in six weeks. I'm not likely to work in six more. When I first moved back, I gave myself to the end of summer to find a job. It's the middle of September now, and the days are cooling off. In another month the leaves will turn.

I was making fifteen dollars an hour hanging drywall in Cincinnati. Gabriel had gotten comfortable in his grade school. Cathy was training to be a nurse.

I think about these things we've given up. I think how Cathy didn't kick when I asked her to move, how she hasn't kicked yet.

A fellow I met at Garrett told me they were hiring at Silver Oak in Breathitt County. When I drove over the foreman told me he'd just laid off three men, but he'd heard that Allied was hiring in Harlan. When I drove to Harlan, I found some fellows in UMWA caps walking a picket line. I pulled up and said I'd heard they were hiring. One big miner with more beard than face leaned in my window. "Hiring scabs," he said and showed me the butt of a .44 stuck in his belt. I got out of there.

Some days I just drive around, see what all's changed in twenty years. There's one big strip site over on the Perry County end of Ball Branch that covers ten thousand acres, at least. One big knob of a mountain they're still honing down sticks up over Highway 80. It looks like one of those buttes you see out west.

I went camping one night just so I could sit on a ridge top and watch their dragline. The site is lit well enough that I could see it working from two miles off. The boom is as long as a football field. The bucket is big enough to park a Mack truck in. It runs off electricity, big generators inside a housing the size of a four story building. It runs day and night, raking up blasted rock and spill dirt, stripping down to the coal seams. God knows how many tons it's raked up. Just the sound of it is like some big monster come to eat up the world. I could run one if I got the chance.

There's rotten wood underneath the kitchen sink, loose stones in the chimney, and gas in the well water. Grandpa's chair, the couch, and some of the porch furniture has mold. I've stored it in the barn because I can't bear to put a match to any of it.

Cathy saw a black snake sunning itself on the rock border around her flower garden. She's had nightmares for three nights straight, seeing shadows and shapes on the bedroom walls. I tell her black snakes are good to have around. They eat mice and chase off the bad snakes. She wants me to kill it. I feel bad about the idea, but I sit on the porch with Grandpa's old twelve gauge, like I'm laying for it.

Cathy doesn't say she'd feel better suited elsewhere. I know it. She knows I know it. I'm not all the way used to this stuck-up-a-holler kind of life myself. Most times I love it, having a big garden to tend and miles of hills to hike and hunt in and a little creek for fishing and nobody around to bother me. Sometimes I'll step out on my porch in the middle of the night and let loose a big yell and feel like I've been set free from the world.

But there's times I wish my nearest neighbor wasn't a mile away, times I feel a little closed in by all the trees and mountains on every side. I'd like to go to the grocery without having to drive twenty miles. I'd like to get more than one channel on the TV without having to climb the mountain and reset the antenna every time the wind blows. I'd like not to have to truck my own garbage to the dump. I'd like to go to a baseball stadium and sit among the crowd. I worry about the only road in and out being so rocky and tore up

I can barely drive it. I know I'll need a four-wheel drive this winter.

Sometimes I catch a whiff of cigarette smoke. It's a habit Cathy was supposed to quit when she got pregnant. I know it's only one or two once in a while, and I know it's just boredom and worry that makes her smoke. I hate to say anything.

Yesterday a neighbor brought us a peck of fresh picked green beans. Cathy cooked them with the strings still in. She didn't know. I didn't mean to criticize her, but I guess that's how it came out.

This morning I brought Grandma's quilting frames down from the attic and set them up in the living room. Cathy's been cutting out squares and studying pattern books for a week. When I came home, I found the frames empty and pieces of cloth scattered all over like they'd been caught in a tornado. Cathy was in bed. The room smelled of smoke.

"I have a headache," she said.

"How'd the quilting go?" I asked.

"I can't do it," she said.

Just before dark, I see the blacksnake crawling along the edge of the flower garden. There's enough light for me to see the white of his underside and to see him flick his tongue out. He lays on top of the rock border for a long time, poses there, like he's not alive but stuffed. When I shoot him in two, his severed halves leap up in a puff of dust and stone chips and flop among Cathy's marigolds.

Cathy comes outside when she hears the shot. When she puts her hand on my shoulder, her fingernail scrapes my neck a little, and I shiver. She goes back inside without speaking, and I know she thinks I'm mad at her for making me shoot the snake or for not being able to quilt or for not knowing to string green beans before she cooks them.

Jerry Everage is one of the few local boys who doesn't belong to the UMWA. I meet him one day in this little road-side tavern just beyond Wayland, and we get to be buddies over our beers.

"I don't believe in no unions," he says. "Them unions is just a gang of rogues, out for themselves. Time was they made sense, but no more. This day and time a man's got the right to work, whether he's union or not."

He's an all-right fellow, but I can see where his mouth might get him in trouble. When he clues me in on a chance to haul coal for Allied, I think first about that big miner with the .44. I think about being called a scab. Then I think, "Hell, a man does have the right to work if there is any." It feels good to tell Cathy I've found a job.

When I get in line to be loaded my first day in one of Allied's old Macks, a picket cracks my windshield with a piece of slate. There are off-duty county mounties and private guards hired to keep the union men back. They've cleared the barricade and made a way for us to drive through, but we still have to run a gauntlet of UMWA pickets. More than one rock bounces off my cab when I go out with my load.

It feels good to be driving a Mack truck, barrelling down the highway, pulling my horn for any little boys that come out on the roadside to see me pass. The only times things get hot is around the mine, when I have to navigate through all those pickets. Some days their wives and kids come out with them and stand screaming obscenities, the worst I ever heard. Little kids and women. But then me and Jerry go drink beer after work, and he talks me into believing it's all right.

"Think about your own woman," he says, "your own kid."

I've set up empty oil cans on the rail fence between the pasture and hay bottom. Gabriel wants to shoot. The twelve gauge is going to kick more than he expects. I hunker down behind him as he takes aim, ready to brace him against the recoil. I sight over his shoulder, see the barrel waver, the gunsight dipping off the can. "Watch your aim," I say, and when I do he lowers the gun.

"I don't want to do it," he says.

"Why go ahead," I say. "There's nothing to it."

He hesitates but raises the gun again and aims. The barrel trembles as he tenses on the trigger. The sound of the shot rings my ears. The gunpowder burns my nose. Gabriel is moved back a step, but I haven't had to catch him. I see a puff of wood dust a little to the right of the oil can, then the can itself teeters and falls off the rail.

"How'd that feel?" I ask, taking the gun and breeching the barrel to pop out the shot casing. There's still a little cloud of gun smoke around us.

"What?" he asks. I realize his ears are ringing as much as mine, but he's smiling and rubbing his shoulder.

We walk over to the fence to find the can and count the shot holes.

"My ears are ringing," he shouts. He's still grinning.

"Mine are too," I say. "That gun kicks hard, don't it?"

133

He rubs his shoulder. "Not too bad," he says.

We count seven shot holes in the can. Gabriel is so happy he hit it that he wants to shoot again. He shoots better each time, and as we're walking home he wants to know if he can have his own gun and if we can go hunting sometime. I tell him squirrel season opens in a few weeks. He gets excited at the idea. I worry how Cathy will take to him hunting or even just shooting a gun. Guns mean something different to her than they do to me. That comes from her growing up in the city. I understand how she feels.

Supper is ready when we get home. We sit at the kitchen table and eat fried corn and boiled potatoes and green beans and yellow cornbread and sliced tomatoes and cucumbers. With all this good garden food, I don't even miss the meat we've not been having. My first paycheck caught us up on our bills a little, but there'll be no splurging for a while.

The evening cool enters the house through the open windows. Moths gather on the screens. Gabriel brags on his shooting while Cathy and I sneak grins at one other. I've not seen Cathy so cheerful since our move. It's like a light has come back on inside her. I know it's from having money again and feeling like we got some control in our lives. We talk about names for the baby and about what we still need to do to the house before it's born. She talks about finishing her nurse's training. She's already looked into a program she could drive to just over in Pikeville.

We go onto the porch and sit listening to the night sounds—the crickets and frogs and night birds. Who knows what all? We watch bats flock into the sky, listen to them squeak as they hunt the swarms of gnats and mosquitoes.

I want to hug Cathy and Gabriel in my arms and say, "See

what a good life we have here." Instead, I just rock real easy in Grandpa's rocking chair and don't make a sound for fear of breaking this spell we've come under.

After about an hour Cathy pushes herself up from her chair. I think how much she is starting to show from the baby. "It's time for bed," she says.

Gabriel and I say "okay" in the same breath, though I linger on the porch for a while, smoking one of Cathy's cigarettes for an excuse. When I finally go inside, I leave the door open, to air the house and keep it cool.

Teddy Sloane is about a third cousin on my daddy's side. I barely recognize him the day he comes to visit. He's bald and years older looking than his actual age, which is the same as mine. He wears a big beard that's like a dried-out bush hanging down his chest, his face framed by black horn-rimmed glasses.

"Don't you know me?" he asks, and I shake his hand like he's my long-lost brother, but there's truthfully not much in his face I remember from when we were little boys.

We visit for a while, then he asks me if I could help him tear down an old storage building on his place. I'm reluctant at first. It's Saturday, and I want to listen to a ball game on the radio with Gabriel, but I say all right. It's the best investment of time I've ever made. I salvage enough wood to fix our kitchen floor and get Teddy to come over the next weekend and help me carpenter.

I tell Cathy that Teddy is the best hand to work I've ever seen. He hardly ever speaks. Sometimes I'll forget he's even there and just get caught up in the job, and when I look over at him he'll be hammering away, never a letup. It's almost religious to watch him go at it.

The barn roof is our latest project. If I'm ever to have livestock or keep hay, I'll need to patch it enough to hold out the weather. I'm for just a quick fix, but Teddy wants it done right.

Gabriel will stand and hold our ladders or bring us nails or dropped hammers or drinks of water. I look up one day and he's standing on the top rung of the ladder with a roll of tin on his shoulder. I hold back telling him to get down. He's not the same boy I brought down here. I admire the change in him.

Some weekends Jerry Everage comes over to help, though most of what he does is drink beer and supervise. Sometimes he brings a little bag of dope that him and me smoke on when Gabriel's not around. He slows us down with all his talk, but what he takes away in work he makes up in entertainment value.

Jerry's an expert on whatever comes to mind. I'll argue back and forth just for the fun of it. Teddy mostly tries to ignore him. But sometimes I'll hear a big sigh or groan over something Jerry has said.

"Man's got the right to work," Jerry says. "It's un-American them unions trying to keep him from it." Same old speech.

Once in a while Teddy will try to dispute what Jerry is saying. I think more than anything he just gets tired of hearing Jerry run his mouth. "I kindly disagree," he'll say. Teddy is so soft-spoken it's hard to make him out, but Jerry will shut right up and listen hard. Then, when Teddy's had his say, Jerry will start back in right where he left off.

It's a relief when Cathy takes up with Teddy's wife. In some ways they're complete opposites. Lori's about as country as it gets. She's big boned and meaty and backwards talking, and she's not been out of eastern Kentucky her whole life, even to go to Lexington or Kingsport. In some ways they're a lot alike though. Lori has the busiest hands I've ever seen on a person. It's like if she can't keep them occupied they'll fly off like birds. That's how her and Cathy are alike. If Cathy's not occupied with something she gets so down on herself you can't live with her. Lori's been teaching Cathy to piece quilts and sew and make shucky beans. They'll sit together and talk and work at something a whole day.

The second weekend of October, we all go over to Teddy and Lori's place to pick apples. It's a sunny weekend. The fall leaves are at their peak colors—deep red and yellow and gold—and every time the wind blows a few more will fly into the air and swirl around.

Teddy and Lori have about a dozen trees of red and yellow Delicious. They've had a good year. The tree limbs are just about broke down with apples, and a bunch have already fallen off. We have to be careful of the yellow jackets swarming around the rotten ones.

Gabriel chases around the orchard with Teddy's two boys for a while, then we all pick apples. We pick twenty bushels from the limbs we can reach, then Teddy and I climb up in the tops of the trees and shake the branches. I almost fall out from laughing at everybody running from all those falling apples. Old Teddy is feeling so good, he stands up on a branch and squalls like a wild cat while he shakes it.

When we pick up what we've shook off, we have another ten bushels, and there's still more on the ground and in the trees. I catch Gabriel with his head turned and let him have it with a big mushy rotten apple. He's surprised at first, but it doesn't take him long to catch on. By the time we quit our battle, we're all covered in rotten apple mush. It's that kind of day.

It's almost another month before things turn sour. One day when I'm riding empty back to the tipple, I run into a state police road block. They motion me into the passing lane then escort me, one cruiser in front and one behind, all the way to Allied's. Just before the tipple, I see Jerry Everage's big red Mack sitting catty-cornered to the highway, like it'd been halfway wrecked. I try to slow down and take a look, but the cruiser behind me hits its siren to move me on. I make out that the windshield is busted, and I'm not so sure but what I don't see bullet holes in the driver's door. I get a little queasy in my stomach.

The UMWA men have backed off their pickets. They're mostly sitting on the hoods and tailgates of their pickups a ways off from the state police barricade. They're smoking, chewing, trading knives to put off their unease. I know that most of them are innocent, but they all look guilty.

The troopers lead me into the main office. The non-union mining crew that was on shift and most of the truckers are crowded in with the foremen and bosses. Everyone talks in soft voices, like at a funeral. We're told how somebody peppered Jerry Everage's truck with an Uzi. An Uzi! How in the hell? Then he just run on off, whoever the hell it was.

We hear some more stuff like how this company doesn't give in to terrorism. How we're all a brave lot of men doing a difficult job. When I stand up and say, "I've done my military service," about a dozen fellows follow me out.

Jerry has already been discharged by the time I get to the hospital. He must not of been hurt much, if at all. He lit out for who knows where.

When I get home, I find Gabriel sitting on the porch with the twelve gauge in his lap. He's so serious looking, I almost grin. I never thought they'd hear the news before I got home. I never thought to call.

Cathy has cried till her eyes are red. She's pale, and I'm afraid she's about to pass out. I worry for the baby. We go round and round for a little while, but my heart's not in it. By the time Cathy's had her say, any thought I might have had of going back to Allied is out the window.

From where I sit on the pasture ridge, I can see just about the whole valley. The creek runs through the middle. The highway runs next to the creek. Houses are situated all along the road and the creek bank, like they've been washed up in a flood.

The sun is just coming up over the ridges. It makes a line as it moves down the mountains, like a border between night and day. The leaves have all turned their fall colors now, and with the sun shining like it is this morning, there's no prettier place on this earth. In another week all the trees will be bare, and when I climb up here, all I'll see is where the hills have been strip-mined.

Teddy says for me to sign up on welfare and draw food

stamps. He says I qualify. Before I do that I'll pull up and head back north, stay with Mom and Dad until we're on our feet again. I could subcontract some drywall jobs or work construction. I know people still. I hate giving up on this place, though. I would like to tough it out. I would like to settle.

Sometimes I daydream about that pony I had when I was a little boy. I imagine I'm riding her fast across a bottom full of timothy. The timothy is almost ready for cutting and swishes against my legs as we gallop through. It's like we're flying, we go so fast. Sometimes I wonder if this is the same place I remember.

There's a dog barking somewhere. I hear the blast of a shotgun—some hunter up early or out late. I smell wood smoke, see it trailing out of a few chimneys. I think how a good store of firewood would cut down on my heating bills. I watch the sunlight make its way in a line down the mountains and think about the day we picked apples with Teddy and Lori and the day Gabriel shot his first gun. I think about the cold of winter to come.

ABOUT THE AUTHOR

CHRIS HOLBROOK was raised in Soft Shell, Knott County, in the southern Appalachian mountains of eastern Kentucky. A graduate of both the University of Kentucky and the University of Iowa (MFA, Fiction), he has won fellowships from the Fine Arts Work Center in Provincetown and from the Kentucky Arts Council. Recently his short stories won publication competitions sponsored by *Now and Then* and *Louisville Magazine*. He teaches at Alice Lloyd College in Pippa Passes where he lives with his wife, Mary Beth.

▼▼▼▼▼▼▼▼▼▼▼▼▼▼▼▼▼▼▼▼▼▼▼▼▼▼▼▼▼▼▼▼▼▼▼▼

This book has been set in Matthew Carter's
revision of his Galliard typeface with
his Mantinia used for display. Set
on a Macintosh Quadra 650
in Quark 3.31 with help
from The Typewright.
Printing by Thom-
son-Shore, Inc.
in an edition
of 1500
copies.